"Don't Look At Me Like That. I'm Not Going To Hurt You."

Megan's gaze dropped to her cell phone gripped high in Shafir's strong dark hand. Nothing about this situation reassured her. "I'm supposed to believe that?"

The frantic vibration of her cell phone diverted her attention. Her messages had come through despite the limo's path through the remote desert. Not a minute too soon! Disregarding his power, his size, Megan dove across his lap, intent on claiming back the phone—her phone, damn it.

Hard thighs of rock-like solidity beneath the elegant trousers were the first warning that she had made a colossal mistake. She jerked her gaze upward.

Oh, no.

Bare inches separated their faces. Megan was aware of muscle shifting under her. He surrounded her. And he was big—much bigger than she'd realized.

Her breath came in ragged fits—yet he didn't appear to be breathing at all. She gulped in air, but her pounding heart she could do nothing about.

Dear Reader,

It was a great thrill to be asked to write *The Untamed Sheik* as part of Harlequin's 60th anniversary celebrations. It's a very special book for me for several reasons.

Firstly, the idea of writing a MAN OF THE MONTH book just blew me away. I've been reading the Desire line for a LOT longer than I've been writing for them, and my bookshelves have plenty of MAN OF THE MONTH books perched up there. They're by some of my favorite authors. I still remember the titles and I know some of the blurbs off by heart. So it's very special to have my own MAN OF THE MONTH story and to be part of the 2009 collection with a group of fabulous authors.

Secondly, Shafir, the hero, is a sheik. An untamed, very male, very primal sheik. Many years ago I discovered E.M. Hull's *The Sheikh* on my mother's bookshelves and devoured it. Mom also had black-and-white photos of Rudolph Valentino, the sheik of the silent screen, that she'd collected. And sheik romances have remained a firm favorite of mine.

The Untamed Sheik also gave me a chance to write Megan Saxon's story. If you missed THE SAXON BRIDES, please visit www.tessaradley.com, for more details. I love Megan's wit and joie de vivre and it was sa great pleasure to find a hero to match her.

Finally, this is the tenth book I have written for Silhouette Desire! Please celebrate with me. To read more about the fantastic 2009 MAN OF THE MONTH lineup, please come visit www.myspace.com/desiremanofthemonth.

See you soon,

Tessa

TESSA RADLEY

THE UNTAMED SHEIK

Silhouette® Desire

Published by Silhouette Books

America's Publisher of Contemporary Romance

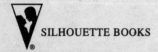

SILHOUETTE BOOKS

ISBN-13: 978-0-373-76933-9
ISBN-10:   0-373-76933-4

Recycling programs
for this product may
not exist in your area.

THE UNTAMED SHEIK

Copyright © 2009 by Tessa Radley

Books by Tessa Radley

Silhouette Desire

Black Widow Bride #1794
Rich Man's Revenge #1806
*The Kyriakos Virgin Bride #1822
*The Apollonides Mistress Scandal #1829
*The Desert Bride of Al Sayed #1835
Pride & a Pregnancy Secret #1849
†Mistaken Mistress #1901
†Spaniard's Seduction #1907
†Pregnancy Proposal #1914
†The Untamed Sheik #1933

*Billionaire Heirs
†The Saxon Brides

TESSA RADLEY

loves traveling, reading and watching the world around her. As a teen, Tessa wanted to be an intrepid foreign correspondent. But after completing a bachelor of arts degree and marrying her sweetheart, she became fascinated by law and ended up studying further and practicing as an attorney in a city practice.

A six-month break traveling through Australia with her family reawoke the yen to write. And life as a writer suits her perfectly; traveling and reading count as research, and as for analyzing the world…well, she can think "what if" all day long. When she's not reading, traveling or thinking about writing, she's spending time with her husband, her two sons or her zany and wonderful friends. You can contact Tessa through her Web site, www.tessaradley.com.

To Mom

One

Silence greeted Prince Shafir ibn Selim al Dhahara as, traditional robes billowing, he swept through the tall, carved wooden doors that a palace aide had flung open at his approach.

The mood inside the king's personal chamber was somber. Three men huddled over a laptop in the center of a round antique table and glanced up at Shafir's entrance. While his two brothers looked relieved to see him, his father—King Selim—was frowning.

Once seated with them at the table, Shafir leaned back, crossed his ankles and met his father's piercing gaze. The king's frown deepened at the informal pose. "You are late, Shafir."

"I was in the desert. I came as quickly as I could." Shafir gestured down to his dusty boots. "I didn't even take the time to change."

As the head of Dhahara's tourism ministry, Shafir had

spent the past week showing an international delegation the adventure tourism and trail-hiking potential of their small desert kingdom. Much time had been spent ensuring that each country's representative understood that opening Dhahara to international tourism meant putting in place measures to guarantee the desert would remain rugged and unspoiled.

"There is a problem, Father?"

"Not a problem exactly." The king's frown lines eased a little. "A challenge."

"A challenge?" Shafir exchanged a questioning glance with his older brother, Khalid—His Royal Highness Crown Prince Khalid ibn Selim al Dhahara, to give him his full title. Their father's idea of a challenge meant a situation fraught with difficulty—one of his father's own diplomats' worst nightmares.

"It is a challenge that should suit you well, Shafir."

"Me?" Shafir raised a dark eyebrow. "What about my honorable brothers? Or have you already allocated other challenges to them?"

Khalid grinned. "You arrived last—you drew the short straw."

"The most honorable straw, and a chance to be a hero." His younger brother, Rafiq, appeared wickedly amused.

"Be a hero?" Shafir eyed his brothers. Both looked like they were trying hard not to laugh.

His father, by contrast, looked grave. "Shafir, you are a man who has been forged and hardened to steel by the Dhaharan desert."

Shafir bowed his head, then lifted it to assess his father respectfully.

Black eyes set in a wise, weather-beaten face stared back at him. "My son, I don't want any scandal, so it has to be one of you three who take care of it. Rafiq is already committed, and his beloved may not understand." The king glanced to his right. "And Khalid is the crown prince. I cannot afford—"

Shafir interrupted. "So what *is* this challenge?"

"It's not that tough." Rafiq clicked open an image on the laptop on the table in front of them. "And this time I wouldn't exactly call it a challenge. All you need to do is get rid of *her*."

An image of a woman flashed up on the monitor. Shafir got an impression of dark hair, plus eyes tilted up at the corners and brimming with laughter. The barrage of questions he'd been about to ask evaporated, leaving only one: "Who is she?"

"She is the woman who is about to derail Zara's fairy-tale wedding," said Rafiq.

"Do not mock your cousin." The king scowled. "Zara's wedding is the first in our family in almost two decades. My three sons have failed to oblige me."

"Our hopes are pinned on Rafiq," Shafir said quickly, and flags of color flared in his younger brother's cheeks. "He's in love."

"But not yet betrothed to be wed." A reproachful glance at all of them accompanied the king's words. "For now there is only Zara's wedding. With the immense media buildup, I cannot let that woman wreck the dreams of our nation."

The glare the king bestowed on *that woman's* image gave Shafir pause. This was the first he'd heard of any threat to his cousin's wedding. But it certainly explained his father's displeasure. The king had always doted on Zara, his dead brother's only child.

Shafir had met the intended bridegroom. Jacques Garnier was a French businessman whose family was enormously wealthy. Apart from other interests, like importing rugs and olives from the Middle East, the Garniers owned a château in the Loire Valley, and Jacques exported wines worldwide from the family winery. King Selim had been highly satisfied with the match, particularly since Zara was very much in love.

But now there appeared to be a glitch. Shafir suppressed a curse and stared at the screen. "What is her name?"

"Megan Saxon."

It wasn't her regular, unmistakably beautiful features that captured Shafir's attention. It was the zest for life that she radiated, her eyes sparking with the same irrepressible humor that curved her lips upward. *Joie de vivre,* the French called it.

Shafir glanced away. "How do you know she intends to sabotage Zara's wedding?"

His father sighed. "Garnier has been abstracted, so Zara knew something was wrong. Then she found missed calls from this woman on Garnier's private cell phone and recognized the name as one of his business colleagues. At first she thought the worst and cried for a whole day. Finally she confronted Garnier."

"And?"

"Ay, me." King Selim shook his head. "The woman is stalking him. Garnier hadn't told Zara because he didn't want to scare her, but the woman won't give up. And now she's coming to Dhahara."

"She's coming here?" Shafir leaned forward. That was a lot more serious than merely calling and texting.

"She called him just before her flight took off."

Shafir blew out a breath in frustration. "So when did he intend to tell us?"

The king flapped a hand. "It doesn't matter. We know now and can sort out a plan. You can call security in, though, if the woman proves to be…" He paused.

"Too much of a challenge for Shafir?" Khalid said, his eyes dancing.

"The woman hasn't been born who is too much of a challenge," Shafir said dryly. "But we need to contain this. No security forces. No police. We don't want an international incident." He thought of the delegation he'd impressed with Dhahara's marketability as a safe yet exotic tourism destination. At his invitation, two members of the delegation had extended their planned trip and were staying for Zara's wedding. Now it appeared the wedding was at risk.

And Zara's happiness.

Like his brothers, he had a soft spot for Zara, and he'd always gone out of his way to try to be the older brother she'd never had. Just as his father did his best to fill the space left by her father's death.

"Shafir, I need you to stop this woman from wrecking the wedding," said the king.

"Tell her that she's wasting her time—Jacques is marrying Zara," Rafiq suggested. "Convince her to go home."

Shaking his head, Shafir said, "If she's come all this way and has her heart set on Jacques, it won't be that easy." But if this woman thought she could hurt Zara, she'd soon learn she'd have to get through him.

"No," agreed Khalid. "She could easily turn nasty and tell Zara a lot of ass's tales."

Shafir shook his head slowly. "She won't get access to Zara. We'll tighten security." He'd see to that personally. No one was going to harm his sweet-natured cousin.

"But she might sell a pack of lies to one of those European scandal sheets." The king shuddered. "They don't peddle truth."

"She could do that." Shafir rubbed his chin, deep in thought.

"Seduce her, Shafir. Then she'll forget all about Jacques." Rafiq's dark eyes were full of humor.

Khalid roared with laughter. Even his father threw back his head and cackled.

Was Shafir the only one who didn't find it funny?

"You're confusing me with Khalid," he countered. "Women cling to him like bees to a honey pot."

"You scare them," said Rafiq. "Your reputation precedes you."

Khalid nodded. "Women want to be courted, flattered. The desert has taken you over. Look at you, covered in dust, your hair wild and sun streaked."

Shafir glowered and ran one hand through his overlong hair. "It protects my neck from the sun."

"Hmm…but that dangerous, untamed aura might appeal to the woman." Rafiq cocked his head to one side. "I dare you to seduce her."

Shafir glared at them. He didn't do seduction. It wasn't his style. He played it straight and fair with women, just the way he dealt with everyone else he met. "I'm not sinking that low."

"Scared?" ribbed Khalid.

"Of a woman?" Shafir shrugged a shoulder carelessly. "Never."

"My sons," chided the king, "there is work to be done." To Shafir he added, "Keep her from causing mischief by whatever means you choose, and Rafiq will make sure the path of true love runs smooth between Zara and Jacques." His father reached over and patted Shafir on the back. "But I want no scandal, hear? The only story I want to see on our TVs or in the Western magazines is Zara's—"

"—Fairy-tale wedding." Khalid rolled his eyes to the ornately carved ceiling.

"Given all the planning, it should be the wedding of the decade," muttered Rafiq.

"Do I hear a touch of longing, little brother? Perhaps it's time you got married, too," Khalid said slyly.

"Married?" The king straightened. "Khalid, as the crown prince it is your duty to marry first."

Khalid resumed gazing at the ceiling.

Shafir ignored the banter. As long as he was off the marriage hook, that was all that mattered. The woman hadn't been born who could compete with his love for the vastness of the Dhaharan desert.

He cast another glance at the laptop. His task was hardly a challenge. All he had to do was stop Megan Saxon from contacting Jacques Garnier long enough for Zara to marry the bridegroom of her dreams.

No problem.

As Shafir's limousine drew up outside the airport, a plane touched down on the runway. He narrowed his eyes. Megan Saxon was on that plane; he'd already received the confirmation from the airport's chief of security.

It had begun.

Jacques had wanted to meet her at the airport, determined to try to persuade her to leave Dhahara.

"I feel responsible," the Frenchman had said two hours earlier, his normally carefree expression bearing signs of strain. "Through business dealings with this madwoman I've created this unpleasantness for Zara. I need to make it clear to her that I love my fiancée."

But though he admired the other man for taking responsibility for the whole unsavory matter, Shafir had shaken his head. "I can't allow that. It's too risky. The woman is clearly obsessed with you. She might make a public scene." Which was what the king dreaded. "Or try hurting you. And what would Zara say then?"

He'd assured the anxious Jacques that he would deal

with this Megan personally, and finally the Frenchman had relented.

"It must be my fault," Jacques had said as he prepared to leave the palace, "yet I keep going over my business encounters with this woman, and I can't figure out what I did to attract this."

"Don't blame yourself. She's a lunatic."

At the relief on Jacques's face Shafir was seized by a surge of fury at the unknown Megan Saxon. Jacques didn't deserve this persecution—no man did. The woman had also caused Zara a great deal of unhappiness and put a huge strain on the bridal couple's relationship.

Now as he alighted from the limousine, he vowed to sort Megan Saxon out. He'd slicked back his hair and taken great care to dress European-style in a dark made-to-measure suit and immaculate white shirt. The last thing he wanted was for her to be spooked.

But his fashionable exterior was deceiving. As the king's second son, Shafir had been allowed an amount of freedom that Khalid hadn't. While Khalid had been schooled to succeed their father, Shafir had spent several years growing up with his grandmother in the desert, attending the local village school and later visiting *bedu* tribes. It was no secret that the people of Dhahara called him the untamed one.

Shafir was anything but a meek, by-the-book prince.

His jaw firming, Shafir nodded to the chauffeur and gestured to his bodyguards in the accompanying car to await his return. He moved with sleek grace as he entered the international terminal. Ignoring the sideways glances of recognition he attracted, he strode across the marble expanse, confident that his determined demeanor would ensure that people kept their distance.

He would meet Megan Saxon alone. She was going to rue the day she'd decided to threaten Zara's happiness.

* * *

The vast space of Dhahara's international arrivals hall struck Megan first. Its high vaulted ceilings were inset with skylights that let bright light filter in and made the air sparkle. Then there were the acres of white marble floors. If she hadn't already known, the airport would have announced the desert country's breathtaking riches.

A little way ahead behind a brass railing, a knot of people—most of them men wearing the traditional white thobes and holding up signs in Arabic script—waited for flight-weary passengers.

Jacques would be there, too.

His text just before she'd taken off at LAX on the final leg of this long haul—"See u tomorrow. Can't wait" followed by hugs and kisses—had promised that.

Megan picked up her pace, hauling her suitcase behind her. Excitement started to thrum in her belly. It had been over three months since she'd last seen him, too briefly, in Paris, where they'd seen the New Year in together before each jetting off in separate directions. He to pursue business interests in the desert kingdom and she back to New Zealand.

Telephone calls and frequent texts were no substitute for face-to-face contact. Then Jacques had suggested they spend some time together. Megan had jumped at the opportunity to get to know such a romantic, caring man better. Fired up by his stories about the exoticism of Dhahara, she'd booked their accommodation in Katar, the capital.

Unexpectedly, Jacques had objected, suggesting they visit nearby Oman instead. But Megan had her heart set on Dhahara. And finally Jacques had agreed to the luxurious villa in the desert she'd discovered. Megan hoped that this brief escape would give her a chance to get to know him properly...to discover whether the interest that had shimmered between them at international wine shows where they'd met intermittently during the past year was the real thing.

This time there would be no rush and bustle of work to distract them. This time they had six whole days to devote to getting to know each other.

Megan scanned the sea of faces as she approached.

A hard, hawkish face stood out from the rest. Their eyes clashed, his a dark, implacable bronze. His expression was tight and unwelcoming.

Nothing like Jacques's easy French charm.

A shiver ran down her spine and she looked quickly away, her gaze moving along the row. A crease formed between her brows as, decidedly uneasy now, she searched again for Jacques. Nothing.

Unbidden, her gaze flitted back to the unwelcoming stranger. He wore a beautifully tailored suit. Expensive—her fashion-conscious eye pegged it as Dior. He wore no tie. A crisp white shirt with the top button undone provided a startling contrast to his honeyed skin.

Megan lifted her eyes to his face and felt the sear of his inspection as his gaze traveled over her. The lightweight gray pantsuit that had seemed a perfect compromise between circumspect covering for an Arabian country and suitable for the hot desert climate now felt incredibly filmy. She should've worn her black linen business suit, the one with the high mandarin collar and the long skirt. Sure she would have boiled. But perhaps then she wouldn't have felt so terribly exposed under his relentless gaze. When his eyes met hers there was a slight curl to his lip as if he hadn't been impressed by what he had seen.

Megan was shaken by the sense of rejection that ripped through her. She wasn't vain, but she knew she was attractive. Outgoing and friendly, men liked her. She didn't usually inspire this kind of reaction.

Thankfully he was destined to remain a stranger.

She tossed her head and stared dismissively past him, renewing her search for Jacques. Never before had his idiosyncratic lack of punctuality irritated her this much. She felt exposed, naked, and she wished he'd been on time for once in his charming life. This time the effusive apologies that always made her laugh weren't going to be enough. More than anything she wanted to hurry to Jacques's car and escape that disconcerting bronze gaze.

Megan sighed, impatient with herself. She was granting a stranger too much importance. Her gaze swept the arrivals hall, hoping for a glimpse of Jacques's lean body tearing toward her, his hair flopping around his face.

No sign of merry green eyes, no laughing mouth.

"Megan Saxon."

At the sound of her name murmured in a deep, unfamiliar voice, Megan whipped around to find the stranger beside her.

"What do you want?" She glared at him, acutely aware of every exaggerated tale she'd ever heard about Middle Eastern males—their chauvinism, and their assumption that any Western woman was theirs for the taking.

Not that he'd struggle to find female companionship. He was handsome in a hard-edged way. Pretty gorgeous actually, if you liked your men fierce and frowning, which Megan did not.

And he knew her name.

"Come with me."

"Most certainly not." Surely white-slavers, however well-dressed, didn't frequent such public places, Megan speculated with acerbic humor. But despite her bravado she took a quick glance around. Reassuringly there were lots of people in the airport. Men. Groups of veiled women. Families. Even a sprinkling of guards in official-looking uniforms. Several people were looking their way with curious interest in their eyes, but they maintained a respectful distance.

No cause for concern.

At least, not yet.

A hand landed on her arm.

"Don't touch me." She used her most freezing tone— the one that made even her brothers back off.

"Forgive me," he said smoothly, removing his hand. "I startled you. My name is Shafir." A brief hesitation, then he added, "I am a friend of Jacques's."

Her anger fizzled away under a tide of embarrassment.

"Why didn't you say so?" The memory of the disdainful inspection he'd given her flitted through her mind, and she hesitated. No hint of criticism remained in those piercing eyes. Had she imagined it? Or had it just been the standard inspection of an Arabian man for an unaccompanied woman?

He gave her a smile, and it lit up his face. Wow. He'd been handsome enough before, but with the darkness banished he was simply devastating.

"Uh…where is Jacques?" Megan stuttered, unable to take her eyes off him, stunned by how much difference a smile could make. He should smile all the time. Or maybe not. He'd be a danger to the ability of any susceptible female to think straight. Although she wasn't about to forget that unsettling once-over he'd given her. "When will he get here?"

"Jacques is not coming."

She tensed again, her eyes searching his face, scared to voice the sudden fear that struck black ice into her heart.

But he must have seen something in her expression, because he said quickly, "Nothing has happened to him."

Relief flooded her. "You must think I'm neurotic. My brother died in a car accident and for a moment I thought…" Her voice trailed away and she gave a small shrug. Nothing could describe the bewilderment, the sense of loss that had followed Roland's death. And she didn't owe this man any explanation anyway.

"Jacques is fine—he's not hurt. He simply asked me to meet you in his place." His voice deepened further, and Megan thought she detected sympathy in his eyes.

"Oh, maybe he left me a message." Megan reached into the tote slung over her shoulder for her cell phone. She had yet to switch it on; the No Cell Phones signs in the customs hall had been quite clear.

"You haven't been to Dhahara before, have you?"

Megan gave the imposing stranger an abstracted glance.

"If you don't have a local SIM card it will take some time for your phone's roaming system to register the Dhaharan network."

Megan glanced down at her phone, noting the turning hourglass on the backlit screen. Seemed he was right.

With a sigh she dropped the phone back into her tote. "Why isn't Jacques here, then?"

"He had a meeting—"

"—With a Persian rug merchant. I remember." Megan nodded. Jacques had mentioned it when they'd spoken while she'd been waiting to board in Auckland two days ago.

His eyes narrowed a little. "Their meeting is dragging on longer than expected. He asked me to fetch you and take you to your hotel."

Instantly her suspicions seemed foolish. If it hadn't been for that initial inspection he'd given her, Megan would have relaxed completely. "Thank you for meeting me."

"It is my pleasure."

Megan allowed him to relieve her of the retractable pull handle of her suitcase. Conscious of his strength and the muscular bulk of his body under the exquisitely tailored suit, she trotted beside him as they headed for the airport's glass exit doors.

Outside, a host of unfamiliar scents assailed her. Spices. Heat. Dust. The hot, dry fragrance of the Dhaharan desert.

A frisson of delight shook her. This was a wild untamed world such that she, a New Zealand country girl at heart, had never experienced. Nomads. Caravans. She couldn't wait to explore it further with Jacques at her side.

"This way." The command uttered in a throaty growl brought her back to earth.

This way revealed a shiny white limousine with a second car waiting behind. A uniformed man built like a barn door leaned against the front passenger door while a chauffeur stood attentively beside the open rear door. Except this chauffeur wore flowing robes and a white headdress that was secured with the black cords that the guidebook she'd read on the plane said were called *agal*. A far cry from the black uniform and peaked cap she was accustomed to. Bemused, Megan ducked into the silent interior.

The cool air-conditioning was disappointing after the hot air redolent with Arabian fragrances. Megan leaned back against plush black velvet cushions and spared a glance for the man who had followed her in.

He dominated the enclosed space, giving Megan the sense of a wild animal that had been temporarily caged. A wolf perhaps. She met those bronze eyes. No, not a wolf—this was no animal that ran in packs. A panther. Or a jaguar. Wild and very, very dangerous.

She stilled, her pulse quickening with sudden apprehension. Then he smiled and the mood of danger evaporated. He was urbane, smooth, a civilized twenty-first-century man. Except for the reflected gleam of those magnetic eyes in the dimness.

Okay, maybe not completely civilized.

Megan shook off the strange fancy. Civilized or not, he wasn't her problem. Thank God.

A need to fill the prickling silence forced her into conversation. "You said you and Jacques are friends?"

A nod. But he didn't bother to expand.

Megan swallowed. She needed to see Jacques again. Despite his family's wealth, Jacques was predictable... easygoing...charming.

Civilized.

Everything this man wasn't.

After drawing in a deep breath, she exhaled. "It was a long flight," she said as his head turned toward her. "How long will it take to get to the hotel?" It would be a relief to freshen up the room she had booked for the night. She and Jacques planned to leave for the desert villa early tomorrow morning.

The man who had introduced himself only as Shafir leaned forward and opened the door of a well-concealed fridge. "Forgive me. I have been remiss. Would you like a drink? Champagne, perhaps?"

So he could produce manners when he had to. For the first time Megan realized her throat was parched. "A drink would be lovely, but I'd prefer mineral water, please."

She'd barely eaten on the flight, and there was no point getting light-headed. There would be time enough for that tomorrow. No doubt she and Jacques would share a bottle of champagne on the terrace overlooking the desert and toast each other...and their hopes of discovering something meaningful.

A small green bottle and a glass appeared with a flourish. The sound of gurgling water filled the space between them. Then Megan found herself holding a cold, smooth glass. A crack sounded as he pulled the tab off a Coca-Cola and lifted the can to his lips.

The dimmed ceiling lights reflected off his hair. It hung to just below his collar, longer than she would've expected given his carefully conservative attire. Below his chin she could see his throat moving as he drank thirstily, his sleek skin gleaming as the light caught it.

Wrenching her gaze away, Megan took a hurried sip of the water. The dryness in her throat eased. Resolutely she turned her head as the limousine crested a rise and stared out through the tinted windows to where the concrete highway uncurled through the desert like a silver ribbon. In the distance the sands undulated in mounds. Dunes. Again a sense of anticipation stirred her.

It was all so wonderfully alien.

And so different from the lush green of the Hawkes Bay where she'd grown up and where—aside from the frequent business trips abroad to wine shows—she'd lived all her life.

She leaned forward, absorbing the view, the exoticism of it all. "That's the Dhaharan desert, right?" She couldn't suppress the lilt in her voice. "Almost four thousand square miles of dry sand that comparatively few people inhabit."

"That's correct. But it's not as bleak as people think."

Scanning the stark, golden dunes that sloped dramatically away from the highway, concealing the city of Katar that lay beyond, she said, "I read that tourism in Dhahara will be expanding in the near future."

"You're well informed." He sounded surprised.

"I was interested."

"Why?"

There was an edge to his voice. Yanked from her study of the dunes, Megan looked away from the gold-shaded landscape. "Why not?" She shrugged. "I also read that while Dhahara does import some products from the United States and the European Union, it's pretty self-sufficient and does very well on exports like oil, olives and handmade rugs." Suddenly conscious of sounding like she'd swallowed a guidebook, Megan abruptly stopped talking.

"What do you hope to find here in Dhahara?"

Definitely an edge and a glint of suspicion in those strange eyes.

"What do I hope to find?" she echoed his question. "What does anyone hope for when they visit a place they've never been? Excitement...adventure...romance." His expression darkened at her flippant reply. "Okay, more than anything I want to relax. It's been a long time since I've had a holiday." *And I badly want to fall in love with Jacques.* But she didn't say that. Instead she asked, "How long until we reach Katar? I can't wait to freshen up."

He blinked.

Unease coiled coldly in the pit of her stomach. She glanced out the window. The dunes had receded, giving the impression that the desert had expanded. "Shouldn't there be buildings...high-rises out there?"

"There are no high-rises in Dhahara. We pride ourselves on preserving our desert heritage—even in our cities."

Of course. She'd read about the determination of the Dhaharans to keep their traditional architecture. But where was the urban sprawl of industrial buildings that lay on the outskirts of most big cities?

She fell silent and scanned the landscape beyond the glass. Surely the highway should be packed with vehicles? After all, according to the guidebook she'd devoured on the plane, millions lived in Katar. Yet there was little sign of human activity, just the odd dot far ahead of them on the highway and even fewer in their wake. Even the car that had been waiting behind them at the airport had disappeared.

Megan's unease deepened.

He'd never answered her question about how long it would take to reach the capital. Apart from what looked like tracks, no major roads branched off the highway, which cut straight through the desert.

The first shard of real fear spiked through her. Polite inquiry had gotten her nowhere, and she'd never been one to avoid an issue. "You're not taking me to my hotel, are you?"

He stared at her from inscrutable eyes.

The fear spread. "Answer me! Where are you taking me?" Stupid! Why had she ever gotten into this limousine with him at all? He'd said his name was Shafir. No surname. And that he was a friend of Jacques. That was the sum total she knew about the man.

What had she done?

"I want to talk to Jacques. Now." Her voice shook just a little. Inside, her heart was hammering against her rib cage.

"He's in a meeting."

The pitch of his voice didn't change, but Megan no longer believed him. "You're lying! Where is Jacques? I don't think you're a friend of his at all. What have you done to him?"

"Calm down." The icy whiplash of his voice steadied her. "I have done nothing to Jacques."

"Who the hell are you?" She thought desperately about everything she'd devoured about Dhahara. It was a wealthy kingdom ruled by King Selim al Dhahara. She couldn't recall reading about any political unrest. Or kidnappings. But then, she'd been excited at the prospect of seeing Jacques again. Her focus had been on the exotic and romantic aspect of the country. Beyond assuring herself that the country was safe and tourist friendly, she hadn't done a lot to find out about the political subtleties. Another mistake. Was he some crazed politico? Or a bandit out for ransom? Or, heaven help her, a terrorist?

Oh, God.

She stared at him, her eyes stretched wide, her pulse pounding in her ears.

"Don't look at me like that. I'm not going to hurt you." In one swift movement he crumpled the can and slotted it into a concealed rubbish holder.

Megan's gaze fixed on the mangled red-and-white remains of metal. "I'm supposed to believe that?" she muttered.

He growled something that she barely heard, too focused on the ruthless strength he'd revealed by crushing that can as if it were no more than a wad of tissue paper.

The frantic vibration of her cell phone diverted her attention from the crumpled metal between his fingers. Her messages had come through—the roaming service must have kicked in, and not a minute too soon! Feeling like the cavalry had arrived, Megan reached for her bag, but as she extracted the phone, a hard hand closed over hers.

"I'll take that."

No way! Disregarding his power, his size, Megan grabbed his wrist and wrestled with him, determined not to let him commandeer her last link to the outside world.

In one simple move he seized the phone and transferred it to his other hand and held it away from her. Driven by desperation, Megan dove across his lap, intent on claiming back the phone—*her* phone, dammit.

The hard thighs that tightened to rocklike firmness beneath his elegant trousers was the first warning that she had made a colossal mistake. She jerked her gaze upward.

Oh, no.

Bare inches separated their faces. Megan was aware of muscle shifting under her. He surrounded her. And he was big—much bigger than she'd realized.

Her breath came in ragged fits, yet he didn't appear to be breathing at all. She gulped in air, but she could do nothing about her pounding heart.

A stillness fell between them.

Danger. Her senses shrieked the warning. It struck Megan

exactly how vulnerable her position was. Scrambling off his lap, she abandoned all attempts to retrieve her phone.

"Sorry," she muttered, unsettled by her rash stupidity.

"Don't be sorry." But he didn't smile. His cheekbones stood out starkly under the tight mask of tawny skin. "Be careful."

Two

Was that a threat?

How could she have put herself at risk in this way?

Thoughts tumbling through Megan's head made it ache as she watched him open the window a crack and calmly dispose of her phone through the gap. She started to protest—then thought better of it. He'd said he wouldn't hurt her. But that had been before she'd clambered all over him fighting him for her phone.

Now she was heart-stoppingly conscious of the hard strength of his body. How could he not be equally aware of hers? Her eyes darted around. They were alone in the dimly lit limousine. What if he decided to…

Not that!

Her mind blanked out.

Megan pulled herself together. Think! She picked up her water to buy herself time and took an unsteady sip.

"Your phone is of no use deep in the desert. There are no cell phone towers."

Of course he'd say that.

Bastard.

Megan didn't deign to look at him. She took another sip of water and started to count silently and a little shakily to herself. One. Two. She wasn't going to respond to anything he said. Three.

"I hate it when women sulk."

Megan forgot she wasn't going to look at him, that she intended to starve him of her responses. Instead she blurted out, "I never sulk."

"Your lips are pursed, and your hands are clenched around that glass so hard it's going to shatter between your fingers." He sighed. "I recognize the signs."

Feminine fury rose into her throat in a hot ball.

Next he'd be accusing her of suffering from PMS.

She turned her head and gave him her most haughty glare. "First you kidnap me. And then you rob me. And now you've become an article in a women's magazine. I don't see that I have to talk to you. You're a lowlife. A thief. Someone should cut your right hand off."

For a moment he sat perfectly still, his eyes turning incandescent with spectacular rage.

Then he moved.

Megan's instincts for survival took over. She flung the contents of her glass straight into his face.

The instant she'd done it she regretted it. He'd abducted her, and yet instead of playing along, she'd antagonized him.

Now he was surely going to kill her.

She shrank away into the corner of the seat, her hands shielding herself from his approach. He was so big, so overwhelming. And she had no idea who the devil he was.

Or what he intended to do with her out here in this ominously bleak, empty desert.

The shock of cold water against his skin registered. Shafir wiped his hand across his eyes and stared in disbelief at the droplets wetting his fingers. Outrage added to the moisture already misting his vision. No woman had ever *dared* do anything like that to him, a prince of the royal household of Dhahara, before.

He moved swiftly, swept up on a tide of anger and affronted male pride that demanded reprisal. At once. Her defiance, her insulting reference to him as a thief, her insistent demands to be taken to Jacques, all added to the emotions that churned inside him. Somewhere in the maelstrom desire was building momentum. The curve of her buttocks in his lap had been firm but unmistakably feminine; she had smelled of flowers and amber, all woman.

A desire to yank her up against him—to kiss her into submission—rushed through him. Until he caught a glimpse of the glistening sloe eyes between the hands raised to fend him off.

Megan Saxon was scared. No, petrified.

Of him. Shafir discovered he didn't like that notion at all.

How had he gotten stuck in this situation? By the devil, he didn't care for the challenge his father had given him. He didn't care for terrorizing a lone woman.

Shafir paused. No, that wasn't quite true. His motives hadn't been so heroic. He'd intended to scare her a little—teach her a lesson for threatening Zara's happiness. But he'd never meant to terrify her out of her wits.

He reached out a still-damp hand.

"Stay away from me, or you'll regret it."

At the sound of her desperation his anger subsided as

quickly as it had risen. Desperate. But brave too. Shafir admired that.

Dropping his hand to his side, he deliberately softened his voice. "I've already told you that I don't hurt women."

"Really?"

The sarcasm caught him on the raw. "Really," he bit out. It was true some women feared him and gave him a wide berth, but there were plenty who were drawn to the danger, the legend that he'd become. He was a sheik of the desert. He was wealthy. And he was a royal prince.

Of course there would always be women.

But he'd never found what he sought.

He'd decided the love his parents shared had disappeared with their generation. Though they'd been fortunate. It could have been a disastrous union—after all, they'd been promised to each other from birth. *Insha'allah.*

He'd managed to avoid such a bargain.

Instead he took what women offered him. Willingly. And then returned to his desert lair without a backward glance when the affair was over.

But Megan Saxon was beautiful.

And spirited.

Shafir examined her through narrowed eyes. Long, silky, dark hair, lovely eyes, and skin so pale it looked like the delicate petals of almond blossom. He'd known she was attractive—the computer images had revealed that, though it had also shown a dazzling smile he had yet to experience. But no image could reveal the full extent of her beauty, or the bold, unfettered spirit that went with it. From the first moment her truculent gaze had met his in the airport she'd taken his breath away.

Fire and ice.

"Stop looking at me like that!"

"How am I looking at you?"

"With calculation. I don't like it."

She was perceptive. And still frightened. The rise and fall of her breasts revealed her agitation. Shafir couldn't help noticing that the top button of her jacket was missing—almost certainly lost in her scuffle with him over her phone—and that in the valley between her breasts her skin was pale and creamy. He tore his gaze away and met a pair of furious feminine eyes.

"Take me back to Jacques."

That was impossible. "Would it help if I gave you my solemn word that I won't harm you?" he offered instead. "That you are perfectly safe?"

For a moment she didn't say anything. Then she muttered, "Why should I accept your word? You told me Jacques had asked you to pick me up from the airport and take me to the hotel. But you're not taking me to Jacques or to the hotel, are you?"

Shafir hesitated for a split second, weighing the possible responses. Soon enough she'd know for sure anyway.

"No, I'm not taking you to Jacques."

Surprise flared briefly in her eyes. She'd expected him to lie again.

"So where are you taking me?" She controlled her fear admirably.

A sudden pang of sympathy for her surprised him. "You won't want for comfort. It's better than any hotel."

Her chin went up. "I don't care about comfort—"

"You'll be safe. I promise."

He ignored her snort of disbelief as the limousine slowed to a crawl and the wheels crunched on gravel. Without giving her a chance to argue, or question his promise, he said, "We are here. You can freshen up and judge the comfort for yourself."

Megan turned away from him and bent forward to peer

through the darkened windows. He knew what she'd see. High castellated walls, curved domes and turrets.

"Good grief, it's a castle."

Before he could respond, the limo door opened. A hand appeared and the cuff of a uniform embroidered with gold braid followed.

"Welcome, Your—"

"Thank you, Hanif." Shafir cut off the aide's welcome before Hanif could give away more than Shafir wanted.

Immediately Megan turned her head to glare at him, and he could tell she'd added yet another black mark against him, this time for inconsiderate rudeness. Even his scrupulously polite "After you" received no softening in her disapproving eyes.

He followed her out into the relentless late afternoon heat. Conscious that the beating sun must be draining to someone unaccustomed to it, he put a guiding arm around her to lead her inside. Megan shifted sideways, hitching her tote higher on her shoulder, and his hand fell away.

"Where are we? What is this place?"

"Qasr Al-Ward. The Palace of the Roses."

Megan balked. "My God, it looks like a cliff face. I've never seen anything that less resembles a rose. Who lives here?"

He did. This was the home of his heart. But he had no intention of revealing that to her. "It's been in my family for generations."

He could see her thinking that if she went in she might never escape. At least it would take her mind off the identity of his family. Not for the first time, he wondered if it had been a mistake bringing her here. Rafiq had thought it a much better idea than taking her to a remote Bedouin settlement. She was less likely to escape…to wander off into the desert.

"Is your family here now?"

"Everyone—except for me and my staff—is in the capital." Preparing for Zara's wedding, as she well knew. He pressed his lips together and waited for her response.

"That's where I should be, too."

She hadn't even blinked at the allusion to Zara's wedding.

His mouth tightened further. All she cared about was getting to Katar to stop Zara's wedding to Jacques. Anger balled in his chest. With every mile that had passed his hopes had been growing that his family had gotten it wrong, that Megan was not the self-centered somewhat crazy woman they'd all described. Now it appeared their reports had been all too accurate.

She was set on returning to the city come hell or high water to disrupt Zara's wedding.

But she'd reckoned without him! He was not going to give her any opportunity to wreak the havoc she'd planned.

"Come," he said, impatient now to have this farce over.

She dug her high-heeled shoes into the gravel driveway and stared belligerently at him. "I'm not going in there. I want you to take me back to the capital. At once."

Evidently no longer caring that she was thirsty and tired, Megan had edged back to the limousine and was trying to open the door.

Shafir folded his arms, rocked back on his heels and waited. "It is locked."

"Give me the keys."

"I can't." He shrugged. "Malik has them."

"Malik?"

"My chauffeur."

"Then order him to unlock it." There was immense frustration in her voice as her eyes frantically searched their surroundings for the missing Malik. "Where has he gone?"

"Most probably—" Shafir allowed himself a smile "—to find his wife."

She stared at him, clearly disconcerted. "What?"

"My chauffeur has gone to find Aniya, his wife. He hasn't seen her for two weeks." Shafir didn't bother suppressing the unholy surge of humor. "He misses her when he is away."

The look that Megan Saxon gave him warned him that she'd like nothing better than to see him burn in the flames of hell.

Megan followed slowly as Shafir mounted stairs cut out of desert stone that led up to the imposing facade of the palace. Entering the antechamber, she caught her breath at the riot of color that confronted her.

Her ire at Shafir temporarily forgotten, she gazed around in stunned amazement. Arches met overhead in a glorious celebration of an ancient stonecutter's skill, with the walls between painted a deep, rich red. Persian carpets in jewel hues covered dark clay tiles.

"This is like something out of *The Arabian Nights*," she murmured, overawed by the patina of ancient opulence. "It couldn't be a bigger contrast to the arid desert outside."

"Wait until you see the gardens."

"Gardens?" Megan turned her head to see if he was joking. But there was no sign of humor in the implacable features. "There are gardens? In the desert?"

His head inclined in the smallest of nods. "Oh, yes. Lush, fragrant gardens with fountains and pools. There's even a palmerie."

He sounded convincing—not like he was ridiculing her. Finally she said, "I'd like to see them."

"You will. But I'm sure you'd like to freshen up first."

A slender young woman appeared. Megan hadn't noticed her before. Nor had she seen Shafir beckon to her. The leather slippers she wore trod soundlessly on the floor even though the robe that covered her from head to foot rustled softly.

"Go with Naema."

"But—"

He was already striding away. Swallowing her thousand and one questions, Megan followed Naema through a doorway set unobtrusively in the farthest wall of the antechamber.

She found herself standing in what had to be a powder room. But what a room. Rugs covered the floor, and the walls were hung with fabric that looked suspiciously like silk shot through with gold thread.

A large, sunken white-marble tub took up most of the center of the room. One wall was covered from floor to ceiling with smoky mirrors that reflected the mass of ferns spilling from ornate wrought iron baskets suspended above the tub. Along the opposite wall was a marble slab set with two basins, folded towels piled on one end.

Naema pulled open the doors of a cupboard set above the marble slab to reveal a blow-dryer, toiletries, toothbrushes and paste, lotions and designer makeup, all still wrapped and sealed. Every frippery a twenty-first-century woman might desire.

"If you'd like a massage after you have bathed—" Naema pushed open a door to reveal a raised bed "—I will do that here."

Megan was sorely tempted. But she suspected that once she allowed herself to be indulged her guard might drop, and that she couldn't allow.

Dumping her tote on the marble slab, she answered, "I'll just wash my face and do something with my hair."

"I can do your hair. Very pretty." Naema sounded eager.

"No, thank you, I'll be all right."

"I can fetch clothes, if you desire."

Her own clothes? Megan realized she hadn't seen her suitcase brought in. "My suitcase…?"

"It has been taken to your room."

Her room? The first surge of relief that she wouldn't lose her familiar things vanished as she made the connection. Her room. She'd been expected here.

The anxiety that had ebbed away was back in full force. What did Shafir want with her? Why had he taken her?

"I can go and get it if you desire."

"What?" Megan didn't know what Naema was talking about.

"Your suitcase. I will fetch it."

"Oh, no, don't worry." But Megan found herself speaking to empty air. Naema had already darted out.

The young woman's eagerness to please was bewildering, given that Megan was here as Shafir's captive.

As she splashed cool water onto her face it crossed her mind that Shafir's reasons for bringing her here might be about sex. There was a moment of wild, raw fear, but then, her stomach sinking in embarrassment, she remembered those moments in the limousine when she'd straddled his lap. He'd had every opportunity to make a move on her then, to grope her, to force himself on her.

Yet he'd chosen not to.

Instead he'd efficiently disposed of her phone, radiating tension and danger. Even when she'd hurled water in his face he hadn't retaliated, even though she'd seen the blatant male rage in those fierce eyes. Instead he'd assured her that she was safe. And later he'd talked about gardens. The man who'd kidnapped her had offered to show her gardens, for heaven's sake!

He was as enigmatic as the Sphinx. With a confused sigh Megan turned the faucet off and reached for one of the thick, soft towels. Whatever he wanted, she doubted it was a sex slave. And she should thank the heavens for that.

So what was left?

Ransom? Could he know her family was wealthy? Maybe he meant to sell her back to Jacques Garnier at an extortionate rate. Did he need money? She touched the veined marble slab. It certainly didn't look like it. Not if his family owned this magnificent palace.

Who was this man who called himself Shafir?

Shafir narrowed his gaze as the door closed and Megan Saxon sauntered into the panelled salon that was very much his territory.

She'd brushed her hair until it shone like the wing of a blackbird. But she hadn't changed out of the gray suit.

Perhaps she considered that that would be admitting defeat. He braced himself to expect another demand to take her to Jacques. Hadn't she yet realized the futility of that? Or perhaps the suit was the only appropriate garment she had to wear, and the remaining clothes she'd packed were chosen for a tryst with Garnier.

He didn't care for that thought, and his eyes hardened as they swept her face with its glowing skin from which all artifice had been washed, making her look more radiant—and less capable of deceit—than ever.

Her gaze tangled with his as she halted in front of the divan where he reclined, his suit jacket abandoned, his legs stretched out and crossed at the ankles.

"So who are you, Shafir? You don't dress like a bandit," said Megan.

"A bandit?" Irritation filled Shafir even as good manners impelled him to rise to his feet. "You believe I am a bandit?"

She tilted her head to one side and examined him through critical eyes. "I'm considering it."

He knew what she would see. Most days he dressed for comfort—usually in a thobe. Today's suit had been in her honor. He'd figured she would be more likely to accompany

a man in an expensive suit. And he'd been right. He knew
what he looked like. Wealthy. Distinguished. Powerful.

Nothing like a bandit.

"Of course, I have no personal experience of how bandits dress. I suppose some dress very well."

Her up-down glance dismissed him in a manner that left
him intensely annoyed.

"Then what makes you think I am a bandit?" Shafir's
soft tone would have warned his enemies that he was at his
most lethal.

But she appeared oblivious to the danger as she turned
away and examined the collection of antique scimitars
hanging on the wall. Her back to him, she said, "Your behavior suggests that you must be a bandit, though I'm not
sure what you think kidnapping me will gain you."

"Will gain *me?*" He found himself repeating the ludicrous words. He, a prince of Dhahara, didn't need anything
that she could bring him. Shaking his head in disbelief, he
said, "Come, tell me what you believe I will gain."

She faced him, her eyes watchful. "Money. I think you
plan to hold me for ransom."

He almost laughed, until he realized she was serious.
And if she believed that she must be more scared than she
was letting on. A twinge of remorse pricked him.

"But that would be an awful mistake. I'm just an ordinary tourist."

At that Shafir did laugh, though without humor, and all
feelings of remorse evaporated. Did she think he was such
a gullible fool? "Hardly ordinary," he mocked, drawing
close enough to smell the hint of mint from toothpaste on
her breath. "You're Garnier's girlfriend, and his family is
worth millions."

"So this *is* about ransom." Disappointment clouded her
expressive features. "He won't pay, I assure you. You're

wasting your time. I mean nothing to him. I'm not even his girlfriend."

Now there was an interesting strategy. "You shouldn't tell me that." Didn't the woman have any sense of self-preservation? "You should be ensuring that the blackmailer keeps you alive by telling me how important you are to Jacques."

She eased away from him without giving the impression that she was backing off. "Thanks for the advice. Are you after a ransom or not?"

"Of course not. I told you—I'm a friend of Jacques's."

"That could've been nothing more than another convenient lie, told to persuade me to leave the airport with you." She inspected him again. Apart from the fancy suit, he didn't look like he had anything in common with Jacques. "So what's your connection with Jacques? Business?"

He inclined his head. "And family."

"You're related?" That surprised her. "Jacques never mentioned having family in Dhahara."

"Jacques and I will be family soon. By marriage," he added, giving her a brooding stare.

Megan pitied Shafir's prospective bride. The poor woman would be stuck with this fierce, arrogant man for life—or at least until he decided he'd had enough of her and divorced her at a whim. No doubt the laws of Dhahara favored men and the cast-off ex-wives were left high and dry.

Did Jacques know how risky it would be to allow Shafir to marry his relation? Did he have any concept of how dangerous Shafir was? If so, maybe he could talk sense into whatever relation of his was going to marry Shafir. A cousin? A stepsister? Megan couldn't remember Jacques mentioning a sister, but she vaguely recalled talk of a brother. Just went to prove that they had a lot to learn about

each other—and Shafir was thwarting their plans of a relaxed, romantic get-to-know-each-other interlude.

"The prenuptial contract has already been drawn up,"
he said, interrupting her musings, his eyes fierce and
restless as they swept over her.

Megan shivered in reaction. He looked driven, and she
shook off the cold tingles that rippled up and down her
spine. Surely Shafir must love his bride-to-be? Or perhaps
not. It might be an arranged marriage. For all she knew
such weddings were the norm in Dhahara. Her pity for his
prospective bride increased, but she pushed it away. She
didn't want to think about her. Their nuptials were none of
her business.

All she cared about was getting to the bottom of whatever
mad idea had caused him to carry her off and bring her here.
And then she should be able to convince him to let her go.

She studied the scimitars on the wall again. They looked
real enough. If he didn't release her, one of those might
come in handy—and that way his bride would be spared,
too, from a fate worse than death.

Her lips quirked.

The sound of the door opening halted her murderous
thoughts. Megan caught a glimpse of the aide from earlier.

"Dinner is served, Your Highness."

Megan's mouth dropped open. "*Your Highness*?"

"*Your Highness?*" Megan repeated incredulously minutes later, when they were seated at a polished table that
seemed to stretch for miles down the formal dining room.
Portraits of fierce-eyed sheiks stared down at her from the
walls. His royal ancestors? She shook her head, trying to
dislodge the feeling of disbelief.

He raised one eyebrow and carried on eating.

After picking up a fork, she tasted a morsel and then speared what looked like a meatball. No point going on a hunger strike.

Sure, she'd read about the royal family in the guidebook that had kept her occupied during the series of long flights from Auckland; but what had she done to merit being kidnapped by a royal sheik? This was the twenty-first century, and it wasn't as if he'd glimpsed her in the desert and been so enthralled by her beauty...that he'd felt compelled to snatch her away to keep for himself.

A shiver ran through her at that crazy thought.

Darn.

What kind of naive fantasy was that?

No, he'd known before they'd even met what he planned to do. It had been coldly calculated, not the act of a man driven by passion.

But he was still a member of the royal family, and that must mean he had certain responsibilities. "Are you totally out of your mind?"

"Do not insult me." Shafir's fork landed on his empty plate. His eyes flashed and again that sense of danger was all around her. "I am no *majnum,* no madman."

But she would not be silenced. "How dare you, a member of the royal family, kidnap me!"

His mouth hardened. "I wasn't dared. And I did not kidnap you."

"Really? Then *I* must be delusional." She raised her chin a notch. "Because it certainly feels like I was abducted."

"No chloroform. No hood over your head. No force. Not even a bruise on your arm." He reached out to touch the skin beneath her elbow and fresh shivers danced in the wake of what was almost a caress. "You came without a murmur."

She swallowed. She should have kicked and screamed.

Instead she'd suppressed the twinges of misgiving, more fool her. "You misled me…lied to me."

"But I never forced you. And I've promised I won't harm you, haven't I?"

She couldn't deny that and gave a reluctant nod. Falling silent, she thought furiously about what she knew of the family. King Selim had no daughters, only sons. Three, she seemed to remember. There was a crown prince, a son who was involved in Dhahara's finance sector and a third who ran the country's tourism ministry, from what she could recall. Past that sketchy information, she drew a blank.

"So which son are you? The heir apparent, the money man or the spin doctor?"

"Spin doctor?" Something that might have been amusement glinted in his eyes.

"Yes—spinning a web of elaborate deceit, convincing gullible tourists to visit Dhahara."

"That would make me the spin doctor, then."

"You're in charge of the country's tourism?" Megan gave a breathy laugh of disbelief. "Well, you're going to have your work cut out for you."

"I am?"

Megan nodded emphatically. "Once people—especially women—hear there's a very real threat of abduction in Dhahara your visitor figures will plummet. Goodbye, tourism."

All traces of amusement vanished. "Are you threatening me?"

Megan widened her eyes. "Threatening you? Of course not."

"Good," he growled. "Then we understand one another. Because no one is going to hear about this kidnapping from you, are they?"

Megan tilted her head to one side. Above his jaw, a

muscle tightened. Fascinated, she watched the ripple of movement under his smooth skin. "Well, my family will have been waiting to hear from me, to know that I've arrived safely. When they don't, they'll start asking questions, and until she started helping me with the PR for the winery, Alyssa, my sister-in-law, was a damned good investigative journalist."

Megan lifted her shoulders and carelessly let them fall again, doing her best to project an image of being relaxed and being totally in control. Perhaps, then, this devil in front of her would never realize how shaky she felt inside.

His face darkened. "You *are* threatening me!"

"It's not a threat."

"But you said—"

"It's a certainty." With satisfaction she watched the way his eyes turned to a flat, dull bronze. Perhaps Prince Shafir would now realize he'd bitten off more than he could chew.

His harsh features came closer, so close she could see every sun-beaten line around his eyes. "You are very fortunate," he murmured through barely parted lips.

Her heart started to thud as apprehension flooded her. "Fortunate? I've been abducted, taken to a remote area of some godforsaken desert, and you call that fortunate?"

"Yes. If you'd threatened another man with exposure, he might feel compelled to kill you."

"You're a member of the royal family, so you wouldn't dare. You couldn't afford the scandal."

His eyes narrowed to slits. "Who would ever know?"

Three

Megan awoke, blinking against the beams of golden sunlight that filtered through the fine fabric of the bed hangings surrounding the four-poster bed.

She'd tossed and turned all night long after that final exchange with Shafir, until a combination of jet lag and a plump feather mattress had lulled her churning concerns to sleep just before dawn.

But this morning her disquiet returned, and despite the sunlight her arms prickled with gooseflesh.

"You wouldn't dare," she'd hurled at Shafir last night. But Megan had a sinking feeling that her bronze-eyed abductor wasn't constrained by the rules of civilized society. He would dare whatever he desired.

As he'd said, who would ever know?

Yet, despite the shiver that had trembled through her at the low words uttered with throaty menace, Megan had felt even then that it hadn't been a threat, but rather a demonstration of Shafir's brand of humor. A not-so-funny, rather bleak, very black humor, but humor nonetheless. Megan was still trying to remember every nuance of his expression as he'd uttered the words when a knock sounded on the door.

"One minute," she called, kicking the covers off. She clambered out of bed and pulled a pair of lightweight track pants over her short nightgown before padding over to the door and unlocking it. She then pulled it open a crack to reveal a short, plump woman with friendly eyes.

Relieved, Megan opened the heavily carved door fully.

"*Sabah ala-kheir.* Good morning. I am Aniya."

This then must be Malik's wife.

Aniya bowed, her head covered by a *hijab,* her hands pressed together in front against a tunic of woven blue fabric. "His Highness sent me to invite you for breakfast."

"So I'm not to be starved."

Aniya looked horrified, her hands coming up to cover her mouth. "Oh, never. His Highness—"

"It was a joke." A bad one perhaps—maybe black humor was contagious. Although she'd always been prone to saying the wrong thing at the wrong time. Foot-in-mouth disease, her family called it. But Aniya certainly looked shocked at the idea of His Highness starving a kidnap victim. And Megan remembered Naema's eagerness to carry out her every wish yesterday.

Could it be possible that the staff didn't know His Highness had abducted her?

"I'm sorry. Tell Prince Shafir I'll be down in ten minutes."

Aniya hovered in the doorway. "Would you like I ask Naema to iron your clothes?"

"No!" At the other woman's crestfallen expression Megan said kindly, "I didn't pack anything that might crease."

"It is the first time that Prince Shafir has brought a

woman here. We are very—" Aniya broke off, clearly searching for the right word "—excited."

Megan gave the other woman a startled look. Did no one think it was peculiar that His Highness had brought a woman to stay who wasn't his fiancée? She shook the thought off. It wasn't her concern. The only thing that mattered to her was correcting the staff's wrong impression about her relationship with Shafir.

She started to assure Aniya, intending to assure her that there was no need for excitement, but then she stopped as dark amusement filled her.

So the staff thought her appearance here was about romance.

It would serve Shafir right if everyone thought she was his love. After what he'd done to her—kidnapping her, terrifying her—the prospect of seeing him writhe with discomfort was too good to miss.

Maybe his prospective bride would find out, too, and have second thoughts about their wedding. Yes, it would serve him right to be dumped! Megan wasn't usually given to vengeance, but his actions yesterday had roused a fiery indignation she'd never experienced before. Besides, the poor woman he was marrying deserved to know she was getting a knight in very tarnished armor.

So Megan smiled, a white, vengeful smile. "I'm so very fortunate."

"Yes." Aniya's features grew animated. "Prince Shafir is so handsome, and so wise."

"Wise?" In Megan's opinion, a man who kidnapped a foreign tourist—a man who happened to be part of the royal family and head of the country's tourism—exhibited little evidence of wisdom.

"Oh, yes. People come from far over the desert to consult with the sheik…and he listens to everyone."

Aniya's version of Shafir certainly didn't mesh with her own. And Megan would take wicked delight in scoring points off him. She wasn't scared of him. She would make him regret kidnapping her and bringing her here to keep her captive against her wishes.

Aniya's voice interrupted her planning. "I will tell His Highness his beautiful guest will be with him soon."

Downstairs, Megan came to an abrupt stop.

Shafir was standing at the edge of a covered balcony that opened off a large dining room to the east of the palace. And he was magnificent, every inch the powerful sheik in a snowy thobe that contrasted with his ebony hair. He hadn't seen her yet. He stood, his hands braced against the stone balustrade, his forearms corded with ridges of muscle as he stared out over the high walls that surrounded the palace gardens he'd told her about, to the unrelenting desert that stretched to the horizon.

Beyond the palms in the garden there were no trees to be seen, no hint of green…nor life.

Hard, brutal terrain.

Already a haze of heat shimmered over the golden expanse.

Megan looked away to where breakfast had been laid out buffet-style on a side table butted against the wall. The loyal Hanif hovered near a tall copper coffeepot, and Aniya appeared at that moment, carrying a platter on which sliced peaches, plump dates and shavings of white cheese were arranged. She set it down on the table between a bowl of creamy yogurt and a basket overflowing with exotic breads.

Shafir turned away from the view at the disturbance and Megan found herself impaled by that fierce gaze.

He took a step toward her, and Megan's nerve almost gave out.

Almost.

She rallied herself. He'd promised not to harm her, hadn't he? A quick glance revealed that Aniya was right behind her. And Hanif was pouring the fragrant coffee into little cups. Good. An audience.

Her lashes fluttered. "Oh, honey, you're already here."

Shafir froze.

Gotcha!

Before she could savor her triumph, he lifted his head like an animal scenting trouble and his metallic eyes glinted. He took another step toward her. Alarm filled Megan and she skittered back.

"Sorry," she mumbled as she bumped into Aniya. But her nerves steadied at the contact. There was safety in numbers, she thought with grim humor.

Shafir prowled closer. "Good morning, Megan Saxon."

Megan searched her memory. *"Sabah ala-kheir."* She dredged up sounds that she hoped resembled the words Aniya had greeted her with earlier.

For a split second something that might have been approval lit his eyes. He inclined his head and Megan relaxed infinitesimally.

"Did you sleep well?"

"What do you think?" she challenged him.

The chair beside her scraped out. He leaned close. Instantly her stomach tightened and butterflies started to flutter.

"Conscience bothering you?" he murmured into her ear.

She stilled, willing herself not to quiver as ripples of sensation rushed down her spine. "What do you mean?"

At this range she could feel the heat of his body, could smell the scent of soap and sandalwood and a hint of some elusive spice that clung to his skin. In her peripheral vision she glimpsed Aniya pressing her hands together, a smile of indulgent delight brightening her round face. No doubt she thought they were whispering sweet nothings to each other.

Keeping her voice low, Megan hissed, "There's nothing wrong with *my* conscience. I'm the victim here. Don't try to make this my fault and blame me for your unspeakable behavior!"

"Be seated."

It was an order. No doubt about that. A reminder of who he was and the power he held here in this vast world. Coming back to reality with a thud, Megan curbed the retort that sprang to her tongue and slid into the chair he held. He'd rue that arrogant tone, she promised herself.

Once he'd seated himself at the head of the table beside her, Megan placed her hand on his arm and said softly, "Could you pass me some juice?"

Muscles tightened under her fingertips. Megan flinched and almost whipped her hand back, but by sheer force of will she kept her fingers still.

Hanif deserted the coffeepot and materialized beside her. "Madam would like orange juice?"

Leaving her hand on Shafir's forearm, she turned her head and gave him a quick smile. "Please."

When Hanif had tended to her, Megan took a sip of the juice before giving Shafir a beaming smile. "I can't wait to meet your family."

His eyes narrowed to chinks of fire, and underneath her fingertips the muscle and sinew tensed again. "Indeed?"

"Oh, yes." She gave a little breathy laugh and hoped it didn't sound as fake to everyone else's ears as it did to her own. "I have so much to tell them."

The man opposite her might have been carved from stone.

Except that his flesh was hot and all too human beneath her fingers.

Daunted, Megan looked away from the unwavering stare—only to meet Aniya's enraptured gaze. From where she was standing the maid wouldn't be able to see Shafir's sphinx-like expression. Aniya looked ecstatic, as if the romance of the decade were being played out in front of her eyes.

Megan's mouth grew dry. Well, she'd taken pains to sow the seeds to create that impression. She couldn't back down now.

Forcing herself to meet Shafir's inscrutable gaze, she said, "I will ask your family what you were like as a little boy." Her lips curved up in a smile to hide the fact that her heart was pounding in her throat. "I'm sure you were a *charming* child."

Once upon a time. Before he became the harsh, arrogant bastard he was now.

The ironic emphasis on *charming* together with the pointed look had conveyed her meaning—though it was quite lost on Aniya, judging from the soft sigh that drifted from behind Megan.

A hand landed on top of her own, trapping her fingers between his palm and the taut skin that covered his arm. The gaze that imprisoned hers was brooding and a flash of awareness bottomed out her stomach.

No!

How could he arouse such feelings in her?

He'd stolen her away in broad daylight, brought her to this desert palace and still hadn't told her what he wanted with her. How could she respond to him like this?

She swallowed.

His eyes followed the movement. "Your throat is dry? Some more juice perhaps?"

"Yes," she croaked, trying surreptitiously to pull her hand free of his. His grip tightened.

He was too strong.

Reluctant to make a scene after she'd gone to so much effort to build this into a misleading tête-à-tête, Megan raised the half-empty glass of fruit juice with her other hand and took a quick sip. The sweetness of freshly squeezed oranges filled her mouth and slid down her grateful throat.

"So you want to meet my family?"

What had possessed her to start this? But darn it, she wasn't letting him intimidate her. The glass hit the table. Thankfully no juice spilled onto the starched white linen tablecloth.

"Yes," she deliberately babbled, "I'd love to meet your brothers, your father…even your mother, to see what kind of woman gave birth to such a man."

His brows jerked together. "You want me to arrange a meeting to satisfy your…curiosity?" Every word fell like a stone into the palpitating silence.

"Why not, honey? Especially since as it looks like I'm here to stay. You're not going to let me go anytime soon, are you?"

Megan could hear Aniya and Hanif adding it all up and coming up with goodness knew what.

Love?

Marriage?

A baby in a pretty pink carriage?

But the absolute lack of emotion in Shafir's expression made her wonder if she'd started something she wouldn't be able to stop. She'd tugged the tiger's tail this time.

And discovered a dangerous beast who didn't appreciate being provoked.

"So how is the babysitting going?"

Shafir had just returned to his father's palace in Katar after hosting the tourism representatives at their final meal before all except the two remaining behind for

Zara's wedding flew out of Dhahara at midnight. The dinner, which had taken place at a fine restaurant in one of the luxury seven-star hotels in the city, had gone well, with all the officials eager to set up ecotourism ventures in Dhahara.

What Shafir didn't need now was his older brother reminding him about the woman he'd tried all day not to think about. He wouldn't have been human if he hadn't wondered what Megan had said at lunch when she'd discovered him gone.

Vixen!

So he slanted a long look at Khalid before saying, "The babe is going to drive me crazy."

Khalid laughed. "We all knew she was a lunatic."

Even his father nodded in agreement from where he relaxed in a leather La-Z-Boy recliner positioned beneath a medley of paintings that included a Botticelli angel and a Picasso clown.

"I'm no longer so sure about that," Shafir said, shedding his suit jacket before dropping down onto the brown leather sofa alongside Khalid.

Crown prince Khalid leaned forward. "Then why is she driving you crazy?"

Pushing his hands through his hair, Shafir said, "I've been thinking that perhaps we couldn't beat the donkey so we beat the saddle instead."

"What makes you think we've missed the real problem?" asked Khalid.

"Megan knew Garnier was having a meeting with a rug merchant just before her plane was due in."

"That's easily explained," said the king with a dismissive wave of his hand. "Jacques says she is a trusted colleague. He must have mentioned it in passing."

The lessons of a lifetime were ingrained, so Shafir didn't argue with his father, but he wasn't convinced.

"And you haven't told us yet what she's doing to drive you crazy," said Khalid.

Shafir refused to admit, even to himself, that the passion that had arced through him this morning had caused him to flee from the palace before he did something he might regret. Like yank Megan into his arms and kiss her until the teasing glimpse in her eyes darkened into the same desire that burned in his soul.

Too many times today images of her seductive smile had flashed through his head at the most inopportune moments, causing him to wonder if he was indeed quietly going insane. Returning to the city was intended to banish her from his thoughts.

But he had absolutely no intention of confessing this to his brother. So he grinned disarmingly and said, "You know how women are."

Of course Rafiq, the romantic, had to choose that moment to return from *majlis,* the evening counsel for citizens. "Ah, so you have noticed she is a woman."

"I'd have to be blind not to notice. No man ever had curves or long hair like that."

But Shafir's biting sarcasm didn't disconcert Rafiq, who chortled. "I did say you should seduce her…make her forget all about Jacques."

If Rafiq only knew. It had been Megan who'd been intent on seducing *him* this morning.

Loosening his tie at the sudden surge of heat that took him by surprise, Shafir unbuttoned the top button of his shirt.

"You shouldn't be here. You need to keep up the pressure if you want the seduction to be effective," Khalid added to the unwanted advice.

"Perhaps it is a good thing for him to be away a while." The king rocked forward onto the edge of his recliner. "Absence might make the heart grow fonder."

Shafir almost laughed. She wouldn't miss him—it was a crazy idea. Megan hated him. And how could he blame her? She was his prisoner. And he'd ensured that escape was impossible.

His too-sexy, too-distracting captive would have to await his return...at his convenience.

"Talking of absence, I haven't seen Zara yet. How are the wedding plans going?" Shafir changed the subject before he got tangled up into a knot he couldn't unravel.

Rafiq grinned. "No problems there. Zara is very much in love."

"And very much oblivious to the trouble this woman tried to cause by coming to Dhahara," added Khalid.

"I want it to stay that way." King Selim fixed his dark gaze on his middle son. "That is understood, Shafir?"

Shafir nodded. "Absolutely." He might be the second son, he might have been given more freedom from duty than Khalid, but he would never disobey an order from the man who was both father and king to him.

Turning his attention back to Rafiq, Shafir asked, "And the bridegroom?"

"What about Jacques?" Rafiq gave him a curious look.

"Is he as eager for the wedding to happen?"

"Why shouldn't he be?"

"He's been a wealthy and eligible bachelor for many years." Shafir raised an eyebrow in a man-to-man way. "You know, perhaps he regrets losing his freedom. Last-minute jitters. Maybe he thinks this matter with Megan Saxon will give him a way out."

"Oh, no." Rafiq shook his head. "He had a lot to say about how very relieved he was that you were taking care of this woman...that the wedding hasn't been jeopardized. He'll take good care of Zara."

"Hmm." Shafir crossed his legs and studied his highly

polished Italian loafers. He'd been poised to give Megan Saxon the benefit of the doubt, planning to corner Jacques and ask him a few questions of his own….

Until this morning.

Because there'd been no mistaking Megan's intentions, except that this time it hadn't been Garnier who was her quarry, but him. It had reinforced that she was nothing but a girl after a good time and a rich man.

The sound of his father asking Rafiq a question about the bridal festivities faded in the background as Shafir recalled the honeyed pitch of Megan's voice—clearly fake—and the silken touch of her fingers against his skin. It had all been carefully orchestrated, but hell, she'd been impossible to resist. The muscles in his thighs had clenched to steel-like rigidity, even though he'd known she was putting it all on.

Though for what purpose, he didn't know.

But her behavior had been the first indication he'd had that the seductress mold his family had cast her in might be correct. And he'd felt a wrenching disappointment because until that point he'd been starting to doubt what he'd been told.

He flicked a glance to Khalid as his brother threw back his head and laughed, his father joining in.

These men were his family and he'd never doubted their wisdom before. The years he'd spent growing up in the desert had underlined the respect warring tribes had for his father.

Yet he'd almost been convinced that his father and brothers had misjudged Megan Saxon.

And why? Because she had spontaneity, a candid way of saying the first thing that came into her head that made her seem so transparently honest.

And a way of arousing his protective instincts so that he'd found himself promising her she would be safe… even from him.

Four

Megan's first reaction to learning that Shafir had departed to tend to business in Katar was euphoria. She had no intention of still being around when he returned, and her initial plan was to commandeer one of the vehicles she'd seen on arrival.

Hanif had smiled when she glibly told him that after lunch she wanted to take a drive into the desert. "The sheik said you might want to go for a drive, but the desert is dangerous. There are many perils for someone not familiar with it, so he said you must not go alone."

Oh, he'd been clever!

"I'll be fine," she said airily. "I won't go far, and if I have a good map I won't get lost."

"The vehicles have GPS systems," Hanif supplied helpfully, "but Prince Shafir was quite clear about ensuring your safety. I will be happy to accompany you on your exploration. And Naema will come along as a chaperone."

Megan gave in. Escape didn't need a tour guide—or a chaperone. "I will await the sheik's return."

Hanif bowed respectfully while Megan seethed quietly. She would have to find another way out.

Her next quest was to locate a computer. Trying her best to look casual and inconspicuous, she sauntered into Shafir's study. A sharp contrast to the rich ambience of rest of the rooms in the palace, this room was clinically tidy. No computers lay conveniently around. And the sight of a power outlet made Megan wish she'd brought her laptop along to Dhahara.

There was no sign of a phone, only an empty jack that indicated he'd cleverly removed it. Yanking open the drawers to his desk revealed nothing more exciting than paper, notebooks and pens, and the mahogany cupboards that ran the length of one wall were all locked.

Megan cursed silently. There *had* to be a phone somewhere in a place this size.

The next day she started to search the palace systematically with no success.

Finally she sneaked into Shafir's bedroom, having put his suite off until last. As she crossed the threshold, Megan was instantly overwhelmed by the stamp of his personality. Feeling like an intruder, she closed the door behind her.

An immense carved bed dominated the space, while rich brocade curtains in deep blues and warm tones of gold framed huge arches that opened onto a secluded balcony. At night there would be a stunning view of the desert stars from the bed.

Megan ripped her gaze away.

Beside the bed a bank of state-of-the-art stereo equipment revealed an unexpected love for music, and a pile of books sat on his bedside table beside a phone.

A phone.

Her heart sang. Despite her curiosity, Megan didn't waste time glancing at the titles on his bed stand. She could already taste her freedom.

Jacques's cell-phone number, securely captured in her phone, was lost to her. Unfortunately she'd never thought to memorize it. But she would call his company—track him down and ask him to come and get her. Then, with her escape route in place, she would call her parents and fill them in on the horrible situation she'd landed in.

But her exhilaration was short-lived.

Although the directory operator was able to give her a number for Garnier International, she discovered a toll call block prevented her from using it. Once again Shafir had anticipated her.

The trapped feeling closed around her again.

It appeared she was doomed to stay.

It took the sight of Naema talking into a cell phone the following day to jerk Megan out of her despondency.

She hadn't even thought of asking the staff if she could borrow a cell phone. Shafir had said there were no cell phone towers and no reception here in the desert and she'd never questioned it.

Damn him.

"Can I borrow your phone?"

"Sure." Naema smiled, but she looked puzzled. "There is not very much credit left."

Just her luck. But it was better than nothing.

A few steps took her out of Naema's earshot. A call to Garnier International in Paris got her Jacques's office number. And that landed her a frosty personal assistant who refused to divulge his cell-phone number, despite Megan's pleas—and her hasty invention of a meeting with Jacques the next day.

Naema looked increasingly curious with every passing moment. Megan lowered her voice further.

At last the PA agreed to get a message to Jacques.

"Staying with Prince Shafir at Qasr Al-Ward—please fetch me urgently," Megan dictated.

The PA sounded even frostier, and Megan was quite sure she'd been dismissed as a total loon. To top it all, as she was in the midst of telling the PA how critical the message was, the cell phone's credit ran out.

"I'm sorry," she said to Naema. "I'll give you money for another card." All was not lost. She'd simply call again once Naema had funded her phone card again.

"Malik will bring me a card when he returns from Katar. He always does," said Naema.

"Malik? The sheik's chauffeur?"

"Yes, he's with Prince Shafir."

"That's the only way to get a card?"

Naema nodded.

Megan eyed the useless cell phone. "Does Aniya have a phone?"

The young woman laughed. "Oh, no. She says she is too old for such a toy. And Hanif refuses to use them—he's superstitious."

Megan thought of the pools, the gardens, the many rooms in the palace that would need maintenance. But she'd only seen Aniya, Hanif and Naema over the past few days. The wide-as-a-barn-door bodyguard must have gone with Shafir. "Does any one else stay here?"

Naema shook her head. "Only Malik and the sheik's personal guards. He's been talking of bringing a new man to help Hanif, but Prince Shafir likes peace."

"What about the gardens? The pools? Who looks after them?"

"There are cleaners and workmen who come—they will be here again at the end of the week."

And that would be too late for her. Shafir would have long returned by then.

Megan waited, but Jacques never arrived to rescue her. His icy PA had probably tossed the message in the trash the instant she'd set the phone down.

To burn off her frustration she had explored the palace, the walled orchard and a hidden garden with its masses of fragrant blooms. Yesterday she had lounged beside a mosaic-tiled pool that was surrounded by high walls shrouded in creepers heavy with exotic blooms. Yet, despite the beauty, despite being waited on hand and foot in the height of luxury, the feeling of being caged had intensified.

Not that she could reveal it.

The first sign of pacing had elicited smug smiles from Aniya and waggling eyebrows from Hanif. It hadn't taken Megan long to realize that they assumed her restlessness stemmed from the fact that she must be missing His Highness. She'd given them a sickly smile—which they'd interpreted as lovesick.

At least, any residual fear at being kidnapped had long since vanished, along with His Highness's disappearance. Now, as Megan strode back to the palace, her body cooled by a late afternoon swim, she was just plain mad at Shafir's desertion.

Yet underneath her simmering anger lay a nagging anxiety that wouldn't abate.

Back in New Zealand her family would be worrying about her, their concern increasing with each passing day. They would have expected her to call and let them know she'd arrived safely—what must they be thinking? One of these days they'd expect her home, and when she didn't arrive, her mother would be going out of her mind with worry.

It was all *his* fault.

And what about Jacques? It was obvious that the message she'd left with his PA hadn't gotten to him. In which case he'd be worried sick, too. She cursed the icy woman.

About to mount the steps, Megan paused. Or had her message gotten through? Had Jacques contacted Shafir and been fed a bunch of lies? She didn't know. And that was driving her crazy, too.

And in the meantime she was trapped in a deception of her own creation. She had to keep up the pretense that she'd started: that she was totally besotted with His Royal Highness.

To Shafir's immense disgust, his strategic retreat to Katar had failed to achieve its objective. He still hadn't managed to dislodge Megan from his mind.

Each evening, along with his brothers, he attended *majlis*—the counsel where citizens sought the help of the royal family—in the great rooms that opened off the entrance to the king's palace. He'd hoped fervently that listening to the problems of others would take his mind off his own.

It didn't.

When a citizen reported that his brother had taken his television without permission and broken it, Shafir thought of Megan's rage after he'd seized her cell phone. Thief, she'd called him. The fate of Megan's phone weighed heavily on his conscience.

Then a villager who had traveled a whole day to Katar for an audience told of how his betrothed had run off with a neighbor. The man confessed to wanting to kill the man who'd stolen her, and Shafir thought instantly of Megan, whom he'd taken against her will and angered in doing so.

Yet he could not condone murder. He counseled the

man out of taking such a path, pointing out that it would not be worth risking his freedom—even his life—for vengeance. Better to let the woman go.

Yet the knowledge that he would not be following his own advice and freeing Megan, that her anger would increase day by day, caused an unfamiliar emotion to flare in his chest. He was not accustomed to feeling guilt or shame.

Even as the last petitioner finished, he had no respite because Zara and her mother swept in with Jacques trailing in their wake. Zara's normally tranquil expression was marred by faint worry lines around her eyes, and even the debonair Jacques looked a little rattled.

Was he wondering what Shafir had done with Megan? Enough! Shafir blocked out all thoughts of his vixen.

As Zara and her mother, an Australian who had fallen in love with Shafir's now-deceased uncle, each embraced the king, Jacques edged toward the tables that had been used for *majlis*. Shafir studied the Frenchman from beneath lowered eyelids.

"I hope you don't have a problem." Shafir glanced meaningfully toward Zara. "If it is a problem of the heart, we should call Rafiq. He is an expert on such matters."

"Oh, no, no. Nothing like that." Jacques grinned, his teeth even, but the laughter did not reach his eyes. He turned to Khalid. "I understand that I owe you my humble thanks for relieving me from a terrible situation."

Khalid said, "You owe Shafir. The king told us you've been having trouble with this Saxon woman for a while."

"Oh, yes!" An emphatic nod.

Shafir pounced. "Why didn't you tell us sooner?"

Jacques stilled. A beat of time passed, and then he spread his hands. "I didn't want it to come out. I was worried about Zara." He flicked a glance to where his fiancée was still conversing with the king.

Had it been another man Shafir might have suspected the groom didn't want to lose his wealthy bride. But this was Jacques Garnier, son of Pierre Garnier and heir to a fortune. And supposedly in love with Zara.

"You should have trusted us," Khalid scolded. "We wouldn't have told Zara anything that would distress her. My father adores her. He would never allow her to be upset."

The Frenchman shifted his feet and his gaze moved from Khalid to Shafir.

"Perhaps I should have told you, but to be frank it's so—" Jacques looked uncomfortable "—humiliating to be pursued by a woman to this extent."

Humiliating?

Shafir thought of Megan, of her bright sparkling eyes, of the softness of her derriere when she'd landed in his lap in the limousine. "I don't know about that," he objected. "I think any man would be wildly flattered to be pursued by such a desirable woman."

An odd expression flitted across Garnier's face. "You think so?"

"Oh, yes," said Shafir, driven by demons he couldn't name. "When she lays her hand over yours her skin is like silk, her voice drops…" He let his voice trail away.

Both Khalid and Jacques were staring at him. Jacques stuttered, "She has done this?"

Shafir allowed a slow smile to curve his mouth as if recalling a memory of intense sensual pleasure. "She has indeed."

Jacques looked positively displeased—and not nearly as relieved as Shafir would have expected, given his protests.

"But then it is to be expected." Shafir tossed the bomb into the sudden electric silence.

"What do you mean?"

"It is her modus operandi, is it not? She has simply

transferred her unwelcome attentions from you to me."
Shafir leaned back, stretching his arms above him, every
bit the satisfied male. "I have become the target of her
obsession."

He smiled. A tiger's smile.

And waited.

Khalid looked stunned, while Jacques stared at him,
bug-eyed.

After the silence had stretched to breaking point, Shafir
said with all the pretence of civility, "It is good that I am
keeping her otherwise occupied. It will allow you to be
married without any interference from a woman who hu-
miliates with her passion for you, *n'est ce pas?*"

"You are, of course, correct," Jacques said stiffly.

Shafir widened his smile further. "Good. Then we are
all satisfied."

"Your Highness."

Megan swayed toward him, and Shafir froze.

The journey back to Qasr Al-Ward had passed in record
time—he'd promised Malik a bonus—and with every mile
his anticipation at seeing her again had increased tenfold.

But this greeting surpassed even his fantasies. He couldn't
help staring at her like a hungry, oversexed boy. She wore a
dress that covered her arms and fell to her ankles in the most
exquisite rich turquoise, which brought out raven-blue highlights in her hair. Her sloe-shaped eyes were outlined with
kohl, giving her a sultry sensuality that stopped his heart.

And when her hands landed on his shoulders, he stiff-
ened as the essence of her surrounded him.

Soft. Scented. All woman.

He hauled in a deep breath and inhaled more of her. A
pulse started to pound, resounding through his head…his
chest…his groin.

"Megan," he acknowledged, surprised that he still sounded coherent.

"Shafir, I...*we* are pleased you have returned." Her fingers trailed along his sleeve, and the gaze that met his was limpid.

Some inkling of sanity, of self-preservation, remained. What the hell was she playing at?

Her lashes sank, dark crescents against her fine translucent skin. He glanced around. Hanif was smiling indulgently, while Aniya wore the same expression she did when she watched the soap operas she adored. A twinge of foreboding filled Shafir as he turned his attention back to Megan.

Her lashes flicked up. Shafir's stomach, already tightened by the dangerous game she was playing, clenched further as the slanted gaze collided with his.

"You have kept yourself busy?" Some imp of the devil caused him to needle her, to remind her that he'd been so confident of keeping her under his control that he hadn't even bothered to advise her he was leaving.

But she didn't react. Instead she said, "I have only one longing." Her fingers walked up the arm of his white thobe, leaving a trail of fire in their wake.

At the wistful tone Shafir found himself conjuring up X-rated images of what Megan's longings might be...and a terrifying desire to fulfil every one of them in slow motion.

In the privacy of his bedroom.

Certainly not while Hanif and Aniya looked on, enthralled at the drama being played out. And it *was* a masterful performance. He must not forget that.

His brows jerked together and he dragged his gaze away from the seductress, fixing it on Hanif. "I'd like coffee please...and for Ms. Saxon, too."

"Of course, Your Highness." Hanif bowed respectfully and retreated, as loyal and obedient as ever.

So why did he get the feeling he'd lost control of his staff?

"I have a yen to find out more about your longings," he told Megan, aware only she would hear the threat of retribution behind his words. He could've sworn he heard Aniya sigh. But when he glanced over his shoulder she was already trudging down the long corridor.

Manacling Megan's impudent finger-walking hand in his, Shafir led her to the small salon and closed the door firmly behind them. "What do you want?"

With grim amusement he watched as she tugged her arm free and scooted three quick steps back. Not so confident without an audience then.

"I'd like to use a phone."

Was there no end to the woman's effrontery? "You want to use a phone?"

She nodded, her eyes wide.

Good, she was starting to realize there would be a price to pay for her provocation. "That's your deepest longing?"

She nodded.

"You disappoint me." He stretched forward and touched her cheek. "I thought your deepest longing might have something to do with this." As his thumb stroked down her cheek and across her lips she gasped, the warmth of her breath misting his skin.

"Or this." He ran his thumb across the soft flesh of her bottom lip.

Her breath caught.

"Or perhaps this." Bending forward, he replaced his thumb with his tongue and slid it over the moist tissue of her inner lip. For a moment she softened at the bold intimacy, her lips parting, and then he felt her body stiffen.

"No!" Two hands came up and pushed hard at his chest. "I don't want that at all… I want a phone."

He resisted her shove. "To call your French lover."

"If you mean Jacques—" she gave him a quick glance

from under long, dark lashes "—then yes. He will be worried."

Shafir thought of Jacques as he'd last seen him, his arm resting around Zara's shoulders. "You think so?"

"Of course. Wouldn't you be if the light of your life disappeared?"

Taking a step back, Shafir said softly, "You are the light of Jacques's life?"

"Yes." But she looked away.

"You assured me you weren't his girlfriend, that he wouldn't pay ransom for you because you meant nothing to him."

"I lied. I am his girlfriend."

Was she lying now? Or had she lied in the past? Either way, he now had proof that she couldn't be trusted. So what else had she lied about?

Jacques had always maintained she'd come onto him. Could it be true after all? Was his family right? Was this bright, sparkling woman nothing more than a manipulative female out to grab a wealthy man, even if it screwed up Zara's life in the process?

Shafir rubbed his hand over his jaw and wondered if Megan had any idea that Zara's name meant light. Or if she even cared that Jacques was the light of Zara's life.

Suddenly he was tired of it all.

To hell with it.

Coming to a decision, he walked across the room and extracted the hi-tech satellite phone from his briefcase. Let her call Jacques. Then he'd see for himself who was telling the truth. Megan or Jacques…or both of them.

He handed her the phone and watched her eyes widen in astonishment. "Call then…see if he comes running."

"Thank God he will come. Not every man is quite the savage you are."

That lit his fuse. "Perhaps if I whistled, you would come," he said softly.

"In your dreams."

"No, *honey*—" he used the endearment she'd flung at him "—it would be both our dreams."

Her eyes sizzled with sheer, consuming rage. Her passion burned him. But he ignored it, his arm extended as he offered her the satellite handset. "It's different from a cell phone—better in the patchy reception in the desert. You'll need to stand by the window or it won't work."

After a second she snatched the phone from his hand, her fingers brushing his, the brief contact causing heat to flare hot and uncontrolled within him.

It startled him, this raw, unrestrained response to her. He wasn't a boy anymore. He'd had more lovers than he could remember, and he'd learned about pleasure from women who treated lovemaking as an art, practiced to perfection… yet he couldn't remember when last a simple, accidental touch had roused so much awareness.

By the time he came back to the present she was already talking, her back to him as she faced the wide panes of glass.

"Mum? I just wanted to let you know that I'm in Dhahara."

He stared at the back of Megan's head in disbelief. She was talking to her mother!

She hadn't called Jacques at all.

Megan's free hand was waving as she talked…telling her mother about the shade of gold the dawn turned the desert sands, making mundane enquiries about her father, the weather, the harvest. All things that mattered in the fabric of life.

Then every muscle in his body tensed in disbelief as she said, "Love you, too, Mum. Can I talk to Alyssa now?"

Her sister-in-law. The journalist. Shafir stalked forward and grabbed the phone out of her hand, clicking the off switch. "Oh, no, you don't!"

Five

"You can't do that!" Megan swung around and glared at him. "My mother will worry herself to death."

"You'd already said your farewells. She'll assume it's a connection problem." Shafir waved her concerns away with a dismissive hand, and the gesture caused his thobe to swirl around him.

"She's expecting me home soon."

"You told her you're still in Dhahara. You're a grown woman. She'll assume you'll contact her when you're ready to leave."

Megan sucked her cheeks in and counted to ten. He had an answer for everything. And dammit, he sounded so reasonable.

"Your Highness, dinner is served." Aniya's singsong voice interrupted Megan's intention of telling him exactly what she thought of him and his high-handed, unbelievably arrogant behavior.

"I'm not hungry." The last thing she felt like right now was food.

Especially if it meant sharing a room with *him*.

Shafir raised an eyebrow in an infuriatingly arrogant manner. "And add credence to the rumor that I starve you?"

Aniya must have told him what she'd said. "So your staff spies for you?"

"Amongst other things. I pay them well." His teeth flashed. "Aniya even acts the jailer on my request."

He was laughing at her, damn him.

Yet the thought of the plump, kind Aniya being a jailer made even Megan's lips twitch. And the sight of Aniya's anxious expression made her surrender. "Okay, I'll join you for dinner."

Aniya's expression eased then broke into a smile when Megan cast what she hoped could be construed as an adoring look in Shafir's direction. But she was only doing it because she didn't want the kind, motherly woman to be upset, Megan told herself. Aniya had probably spent hours preparing the food.

Megan tripped behind Shafir to where a table was laid for two in an alcove tucked cozily under a deep Moorish arch.

Wooden latticed casements had been flung open to let in the evening air, and from up here Megan could see the magnificent gardens she'd spent the past few days exploring. From the perfume garden, the rich scent of gardenia mingled with jasmine wafted upward, along with other exotic fragrances that she couldn't identify.

A manservant, not Hanif—a younger man, who must've returned from the city with Shafir—padded in and placed a hand-painted steaming dish alongside smaller dishes of assorted vegetables. Despite claiming not to be hungry, her stomach gave a plaintive grumble.

Then the young man retreated in even greater silence, leaving Megan and Shafir alone.

It was a departure from the previous nights when Megan had been seated in the great dining hall and tended to by Aniya and Hanif, who had leapt to serve her every time she lifted a hand. She had all but begged them to leave her in peace. After her own riotous family—who gabbled incessantly at mealtimes while poor Ivy, the family housekeeper, tried to keep everyone in line—all the expectant silence and hovering attention had been a bit much. But her pleas had fallen on deaf ears.

Now, contrarily, she wished for their presence.

But at least their absense freed her from the pretense that she'd begun. There was no need to flirt with Shafir... and watch his eyes narrow alarmingly as she touched him.

Shafir passed her a dish, breaking into her thoughts.

"What is that?"

"*Bamia,* a stew of baby okra and lamb in a tomato base."

"Sounds delicious." Megan served herself and started to dig in and found that it was. The okra was tender and there was a hint of coriander, too.

"This is *fattoush.*"

She glanced at the mix of chopped cucumber, tomato and shredded mint topped with golden toasted croutons that he offered. "Yes, I had it last night."

"I am surprised Aniya prepared it again so soon."

"I told Hanif I liked it." It touched her that his staff had gone to the trouble of preparing a dish for which she had expressed appreciation.

"Oh." He examined her.

How she wished she could read the thoughts behind Shafir's narrowed bronze gaze. Would he appreciate Aniya and Hanif's consideration for his guest? Or would he berate them for trying to make her comfortable?

That led her back to the question that had dominated her thoughts while he was gone. "Don't you think it's time you told me why you're keeping me here?"

He gazed at her without blinking.

She gave an impatient sigh and set down her fork. "Oh, come on, Shafir, this has gone on too long now. Don't I deserve to know?"

More silence.

Finally Megan threw up her hands. "Don't answer, then. I'll talk…tell you what I think. I had a lot of spare time to puzzle on it while you were gone."

Shafir had stopped eating, so at least she had his undivided attention.

"You don't intend to harm me."

"What has convinced you of that?"

Megan lifted her eyes to the ceiling. "Praise be to Allah, His Highness speaks."

"Don't blaspheme." But his mouth had softened and she could swear there was a twinkle in his eyes.

"Your staff convinced me. Aniya, Naema and Hanif treat me with great respect," she elaborated. "They behave as though I'm an honored guest in a five-star hotel, granting my every whim."

He inclined his head. "I am pleased to hear you have been satisfactorily looked after."

"That's just the point."

"You haven't been well looked after?"

"No, not that." Megan glared at him in exasperation. Thanks to her machinations, his staff thought her a very special female "friend" of the sheik's.

It made her wonder about the woman Shafir was supposed to be marrying. The woman who would link him by marriage to Jacques.

Over the past few days Megan had come to the conclusion that the marriage had to be an arranged one, since his staff had clearly never met—perhaps didn't even know about the existence of—his fiancée.

Which meant Shafir couldn't possibly love her.

And that was a tragedy in the making.

"What are you thinking?"

Megan blinked. "Nothing."

She couldn't possibly admit she'd been thinking how awful it would be for him to be trapped in a loveless relationship. It probably wouldn't worry him—he could marry as many wives as he wanted, couldn't he? And why was she wasting her emotions fretting about his love life anyway? It wasn't as if he was a friend, or someone she cared about.

Dragging her mind back to the important issue, she said, "The only explanation that makes sense is that you kidnapped me to extort ransom from Jacques."

"That makes sense?" His mouth slanted. "I'm a member of the royal household, and the royal coffers have plenty of gold. Why would I need to ransom you?"

His mockery irked her. "It makes perfect sense if you need money but your family doesn't know that."

The twist to his mouth flattened. Her theory hadn't pleased him. She could see that in those very unamused eyes.

She decided to nudge him a little more. "Maybe you have a habit you need money for."

"A habit?"

She nodded. "Not the garment, like a nun wears," she explained, the ridiculous picture of Shafir in a black habit making her suppress a smile. "It means something you do that has become a problem. Do you gamble? Are you in debt?"

"I know what a habit is. I can't believe—"

"What? That someone found out the truth? Is that why you disappeared for the past few days? To gamble 24/7?"

The look he blasted at her was just plain furious. Uh-oh.

Maybe she should've kept her mouth shut. Maybe he was a drug addict. Or an arms dealer.

She shivered.

"I do not need money. Understand?"

She nodded, rapidly, and didn't say a word.

Keep your mouth shut, Megan, she told herself.

But that didn't seem to appease him, either.

He glowered at her. "So?"

So? What did he mean *so?* She hesitated. "Could I have some of that, please?" She pointed to a bowl containing *muhammar,* a mixture of sweet rice and dates.

For a moment his eyes smoldered. Then he shook his head. "You accuse me of…" Words seemed to desert him. "And now you want more food?"

He pressed his lips together as if he were fighting an unexpected urge to laugh, and his eyes turned to a bright burnished bronze.

"Please."

Megan felt a lot better. He wasn't angry anymore. He hadn't even flung in her face her initial stand that she wasn't hungry. And suddenly she was quite, quite sure that Shafir would never harm her.

And that he wasn't an arms dealer or a gunrunner, either.

He might be hard, but she'd stake her life on it that he was honorable. He couldn't possibly make money out of human misery.

After that Megan relaxed. It was easy to ask him about the kind of music he enjoyed, to talk about the latest novels they'd read, and from there the conversation shifted to a photographic exhibition they'd both seen. When he talked his eyes glowed and he forgot to be reserved and arrogant, and he gestured with his beautiful hands to make a point.

He fascinated her.

He was such a complex mix of seemingly irreconcilable

opposites. The desert sheik, the man who could wear a designer suit with panache yet seemed much happier wearing traditional robes—which Megan had to concede suited him to perfection.

By the time Hanif arrived with a copper pot and small cups to serve coffee, Megan was replete…and strangely content. For once she didn't manufacture an opportunity to flirtatiously brush his hand and act the lover. She simply relaxed.

"Oh, I couldn't eat another thing," she protested after Hanif had gone and Shafir held out a bowl filled with slices of halva.

"Try it. It's delicious."

"I know." She gave the sweet a longing look. "But I'm too full."

He picked a small piece up in his fingers and popped it into his mouth. "Mmm…"

She watched, wishing she hadn't declined. He must've read her thoughts because he picked up another piece and lifted it to her lips. "One taste."

Megan suppressed a moan. She opened her mouth and the halva melted against her tongue.

His eyes held hers as she savored the sweet taste, the crumbly texture. She saw his pupils darken and his whole body stilled.

"That was delicious." She strove for matter-of-factness but the words sounded husky…and far too sexy.

Sexy? Oh, God.

She closed her eyes in despair. What was she doing?

"Would you like to join me for a walk in the gardens?"

Her eyes shot open. Why was he asking? Did he think she'd be more…susceptible to seduction out in the dusk?

Then she mentally shook herself. They were alone in an intimate alcove yet he hadn't tried anything. Even though he must've read...whatever in her eyes while she'd eaten that damned halva.

"Yes." Suddenly desperate to get out of the cozy, confined space, Megan pushed her chair back and stood.

Once they'd stepped outside into the golden glow of the evening, Megan found she could breathe again.

A serene stillness settled like gossamer silk around them. Overhead the sky was shaded in hues of deep rose, fading to amber beyond the high stone walls where the last fingers of sunlight beckoned.

"It's beautiful." Megan sighed. "It makes one forget how harsh the desert can be."

"And how dangerous to the unwary."

Megan shot him a quick look. Was that a warning? His harsh features could have been hewn out of the same rock from which the palace had been built. No hint of softness, as harsh and dangerous as the land that surrounded the high walls.

Wrenching her gaze away, Megan walked forward into a walled garden where honeysuckle spilled down the walls, giving the evening air an exotic, pungent scent. She'd spent many hours in here, reading and thinking, while he'd been gone.

"Not all of it is like that." She stopped beside a fountain where water bubbled, the spray moistening her skin, blissful in the dry heat. "There's no danger or harshness here."

"I would've thought that you'd considered this particular garden the cruelest and harshest place of all."

"What do you mean?"

There was a peculiar expression in his eyes. "It's walled for a reason."

"What reason?" Even as she asked a sinking sensation dropped through the pit of her stomach.

"It was to this palace that my ancestors brought the women they had captured."

"Sex slaves?"

He cocked his head. "And this walled perfume garden and the adjoining orchard—"

"—Was part of the harem!"

She'd spent so much time here. If she'd imagined…

"How did you guess?"

"The walls," she said simply. "And the fact that I could wander here when so many other areas I could see from upstairs are closed off and clearly off-limits."

"The best parts are in the harem, though—like the Garden of Pools that's been there for hundreds of years."

"The Palace of Roses…shouldn't it be called the Pleasure Palace?"

"That is exactly what it was originally."

Her stomach turned. "And the women? The ones your ancestors kept imprisoned here? What happened to them?"

"Many of them lived long and happy lives."

"I don't believe it!"

He shrugged. "There are journals that survived. One or two have been translated into English if you care to read them."

"No." She recoiled.

"Strange." He pinned her with the gaze she'd once considered so fierce. "I hadn't realized you were narrow-minded."

"I am not narrow-minded." She forced the words through tight lips until his gaze dropped to her mouth and studied it with careful deliberation.

Instantly prickles of bewildering sensation filled her.

"Then why do you withdraw when you have the chance to discover more?"

Was that what she was doing? Megan examined her reactions. He hadn't threatened her. Their surroundings were gorgeous, and he could have left her in ignorance. Yet he'd chosen to tell her the truth about their origins.

She wasn't one of those poor women. That was in the past. She was very much her own woman. Strong. Determined. Independent. And reading about the lives those long-dead women had led would be interesting. It certainly couldn't threaten her.

"I'm sure the women were brainwashed," she retorted with a shrug. "But you can send a book up with Naema later if you like. I might read it."

He nodded and hooded that penetrating gaze.

To her annoyance Megan felt cheated. Cheated that he hadn't reacted with smug glee to her concession, that he hadn't insisted she must read the memoir she'd said he could send up. If he'd done either it would have been easy to dismiss him as a controlling jerk.

Instead he led her away from the fountain and stopped beneath an ancient, wizened tree with a thick, knotted trunk. "Legend has it that this olive tree was brought to Dhahara by Phoenician traders."

"That would make it…" Megan tried to calculate the age of the tree.

"Over 1,500 years old."

"Goodness." She stared at the tree. "Has it been carbon-tested…or whatever they do to work out the age of a tree?"

He shook his head. "No. We've spoken about it, but my grandmother told me her mother never wanted the legend debunked." He spread his hands. "And what does it matter how old the tree turns out to be? It's the idea that matters—that it has survived here in this place through centuries and watched untold generations come and go."

"That's amazing."

"There are other more amazing stories about the gardens, too," Shafir said as he led her past a row of almond trees, crowned with pretty pink-and-white blossoms.

"They're a work of art. Who started them?"

"One of my ancestors, King Aziz, for his new wife. It is said that she was Persian and she missed the lushly planted terraces, the hanging gardens, where she'd grown up."

"So this was all done for one woman?"

"Yes." He led her deep into the heart of the perfumed garden. "Tell me what you see."

"Rosebushes. Lots of them."

"What kind of roses?"

Walking around the nearest bush with its crimson roses, Megan studied it carefully. The throats of the roses were a dark, rich pink while the outer edges of the petals were the deepest red. The blooms on the next bush were identical. A sweet scent hung in the air, and in the stillness of the dusk she could still hear the hum of bees.

"It's not a trick question. Just tell me what you see."

"All the roses look the same to me."

"Exactly." Shafir gave her a satisfied smile that turned her stomach to liquid. "They're all descendants of the original bush that was brought by the bride, Farrin, when she traveled from Persia to Dhahara to marry King Aziz. This was his favorite palace. He spent most of his life in the surrounding desert. He used to take his new wife with him on his trips out to the nomadic tribes, and when they returned he would help her to design, expand and plant a new piece of garden."

"Qasr Al-Ward. The Palace of Roses, you said on the first day. And these must be the roses for which it is named."

Shafir nodded and leaned forward to pick a bloom. Straightening, he held it out to her. "Smell."

She took it from him and sniffed deeply. "It's glorious."

"The sight and scent of the rose reminded Farrin of

home. But it was also a symbol of love and commitment...
a pledge of what she felt for the man she'd given up her
family and homeland for."

"Yes, but she wouldn't have had much choice. Surely it
was an arranged marriage?"

"That is true. But sometimes such marriages are best."

An alien ache settled in the vicinity of her heart. Would
Shafir grow to love his wife?

Megan raised an eyebrow at him. "Did he feel the same
way about Farrin as she did about him?"

Shafir's gaze was fixed on the rose she held. "Oh,
yes," he said softly. "He wrote that she was the wife of
his desert heart. She was his *ain*—the spring that feeds
the desert."

The words stroked her like a soft, warm wind and
Megan quivered. "That's so romantic."

"Sometimes there is just pure beauty."

"And no harsh and terrible cruelty?"

"Exactly."

"I suppose he died soon after she arrived...or she died
in childbirth? Such stories always seem to have a bitter-
sweet ending."

A gleam of appreciation lit his eyes. "No, they both
lived long and happy lives."

"While she shared him with all the occupants of the
harem." Megan gestured to the space around them.

"It is said that one woman gave him the pleasure thou-
sands could not. She was the woman who made him forsake all others."

"Now that is impressive."

Shafir's lips curved up. "Finally you're impressed."

There was a charged silence as her eyes held his. "Will
you be able to do that?"

"Forsake all women for one?"

"Yes."

"The day I marry, my wife will know she is the only one." There was an intensity in his gaze. "And you? Could you forsake all men for only one, Megan?"

She paused before responding, unable to prevent a flutter of envy for his bride. Then she said, "If I loved him enough, yes—with ease."

"Have you ever loved enough?"

Megan wanted to laugh dismissively, to tell him to mind his own darn business. But she couldn't bring herself to break the invisible bond between them.

"Well?"

"I'm thinking." No one came close. She thought about her brothers. None of them would hesitate for a moment. They'd all found that forsake-all-others kind of love. But she hadn't.

Not yet.

Jacques...

The moment seemed wrong to think of Jacques, of her determination to fall in love with him. Yet he'd seemed so right. He was courteous; he strove so hard to please her. And, like her, his family was devoted to their vineyards. It should've been the perfect match.

But confronted by Shafir's question she wondered whether loving Jacques would ever be enough.

"And?"

Megan gave a sigh. "No, I haven't found that person yet."

She slid her gaze to him. He was fierce and uncompromising. A savage. A desert sheik. A kidnapper. She should have had nothing in common with him.

But beneath all the differences dividing them lay a thread of empathy that united them...and that bewildered her.

Which made her hugely curious about the woman he was engaged to. Megan had spent the evening with him, talking about everything under the sun, yet not once had he mentioned his impending marriage.

"Where will this marriage take place?"

Darkness had fallen like a velvet cloak over them. Megan could smell orange blossoms and an unidentifiable exotic fragrance that was growing stronger. The desert air whispered against her bare arms as she waited for him to say something, anything, that would break the tension that expanded within her until she could barely breathe.

And he felt it, too.

It was there in the way the last glimmer of light shifted in his bronze eyes, the way he held himself very, very upright.

"Well?" She echoed his earlier comment. But it came out breathy rather than slightly mocking as she'd intended.

"All the marriages of the royal family are solemnized in Katar." Then he moved sleekly, like the big dangerous cats he so often reminded her of, his body solid and compact.

She backed up, but branches of an orange tree stopped her from retreating farther. Something in his eyes warned her of his intention. "I don't think—"

"Don't think." His head came closer. There was a split second where she knew she could have stopped him if she'd wanted to. But she didn't.

And he kissed her.

It was incredibly erotic. His mouth moved on hers and heat streaked through her. Lust. Or was it desire? She'd just started to kiss him back when he lifted his head.

The emotions that swirled through her then were even more confusing. She hadn't wanted him to stop. She'd loved the headlong rush of excitement.

As his head descended a second time her heart thudded in her throat. His warm breath whispered against her lips, and Megan knew he was about to kiss her again.

One hand cupped the back of her head, holding her in

place. The other stroked down her back until it paused at the indent at the base of her spine. He pressed her closer.

Megan moaned as his hard body imprinted itself on hers, the silk of her long dress forming a thin veil to the heat of his body under the thobe. She craved the kiss that was coming.

But it was wrong.

And as their lips connected, her guilt won out.

Shuddering, she put two hands against his chest and shoved him back. Hard. Then she ripped herself out of his arms, out of the tangled hold of the orange tree. "How could you do that?"

"Do what?"

"Kiss me!" An anger fueled by disappointment, betrayal, by a torrent of complex emotions she couldn't identify ripped through her. A burning, scalding anger.

It was then that Megan realized why she was so mad. It was either that or cry, dammit.

And she refused to cry. Not because of him. And certainly not in front of him.

"What's wrong?"

She was going to hit him. "You're such a chauvinist. You don't even know that?"

How could she ever have kissed such a jerk back?

He stared at her as if she'd gone crazy. Maybe she had. What other explanation was there for kissing him back?

"Why are you so upset?"

"You can ask that?" She wiped the back of her hand across her eyes and glared at him, wishing she'd denied she was upset. That implied this mattered.

"You never shed a tear when you discovered I had no intention of taking you to your city hotel—not even when you were terrified. So, yes, of course I'm asking."

"You kissed me!"

"So?"

He appeared gloriously unconcerned by her accusation. Megan wanted to murder him. If one of those scimitars had been handy, he wouldn't have stood a chance. "You shouldn't have."

"Why not? We both wanted it."

She didn't dare touch the second part of his statement, confining herself to, "I don't mess around with other women's men, so since you're getting married that makes you pretty much off-limits. And I don't care if it's an arranged match."

As the long silence stretched out Megan found herself getting more and more worked up.

She despised herself for participating in that kiss. She'd never done anything like that before. Thankfully she didn't know his wretched fiancée, otherwise she'd feel even worse—if that were possible. Though she'd like to be able to tell the unsuspecting woman what a skunk he was and save her from a life of misery.

Finally he said, "I'm getting *what?*"

"Married. To your bride. The woman you should be forsaking all others for—even before your marriage is solemnized in Katar."

"Shouldn't I know about this marriage?"

"Oh, please. You're saying you don't know you're getting married?"

He shook his head. "Who told you this?"

"You did." Now she did feel as if she'd lost her mind.

"*I* did?" He stared. "When exactly did I say such a thing?"

"You told me that…" She searched her memory for the exact words. "You said you and Jacques will be family soon. By marriage."

He gave her a very strange look. "So you believed that meant I was getting married?"

"Well, yes, of course. What else could you have meant?"

"I was speaking of Jacques's marriage," he said very quietly into the stillness of the night.

Six

"*Jacques?*"

Standing dead still in the middle of the garden surrounded by the tantalizing scent of orange and almond blossoms, Shafir watched her struggle to put it all together.

"*My* Jacques?" she said at last.

A wave of sheer masculine possessiveness swept him. "Not your Jacques," he bit out, reeling from the edgy resentment. "Garnier is to marry *my* cousin, Zara."

She looked shaken.

I don't mess around with other women's men, so since you're getting married, that makes you off-limits. The implication of that was that Megan hadn't known Garnier was engaged when she came to Dhahara, that she hadn't come to cold-bloodedly wreck the wedding. He badly wanted to believe that she bore Zara no malice. But he couldn't afford to be wrong, not with Zara's happiness at stake. How could he blacken Jacques in Zara's eyes until he was certain

Megan was telling the truth? This might simply be another very accomplished piece of acting designed to take him in.

"Jacques can't—" She broke off.

Then her head came up and her eyes glinted with some emotion he could not read in the dimness. "Why should I believe a word you say, Shafir? Your behavior up till now has hardly been exemplary." But her voice was thin.

In the half light he saw the movement as her hands came up and brushed her hair back off her face. A spray of white blossoms stood out against her midnight hair. He reached out to remove the trapped blooms, but she flinched away and the twig fell to the ground.

"Jacques wouldn't do this to me." Her hands dropped to her sides and curled into fists.

If this was an act, it was a damn good one. He squashed the urge to take those hands, to hold and rub them until they relaxed. Her shock had to be real…or she deserved a solid-gold Oscar. Yet he couldn't set aside his lingering doubts, based on her falsely loving behavior when he'd arrived home—a performance his staff had lapped up. By Allah, he almost had, too.

No, this, too, had to be an act. Shafir couldn't stop his lip curling as he said, "You know Garnier so well that you can predict what he would or wouldn't do?" It came out with an edge.

Her eyes glittered in the darkness of the desert night. "I know that Jacques is a gentleman. He would never steal— or kidnap a woman."

Anger rose quickly at the personal attack. "I'll tell you what I think. I think you saw Jacques Garnier as a great opportunity to land yourself a wealthy man."

"That's rubbish! Jacques and I had something special. He was courting me."

Shafir forced himself to calm down, to think through

what she was telling him. It wasn't true, of course... What was he missing?

"Courting you?" Shafir started to shake his head in denial. But even as he did another possibility struck him. Perhaps it was not an act at all. Perhaps Megan had misinterpreted Jacques's gallant manner and good manners to mean something more and had built a romantic dream from a few flowery phrases. He gave a short laugh. "You've misinterpreted his intentions."

"Don't patronize me! I know when a man is interested in me. I don't need your opinions. You're nothing but a savage."

Shafir's eyes narrowed dangerously. It was a look that anyone who knew him well would have taken as a warning. Even under the cover of darkness Megan seemed to realize that she'd said too much, for she instantly said, "I've had enough. I want to go to my room."

He grabbed her arm as she swung away. "I have not dismissed you yet."

"I don't need your permission to leave." Her voice was tight with displeasure.

"Yes, you do." She had riled him. He would have to watch that. He could not allow her to weaken him in any way. He pulled her to him. Her feet trampled the spray of orange blossoms that had fallen and a burst of incongruous sweetness filled the air.

Shafir dug into the pocket of his robe, searching for his satellite phone, then held it out to her. In a softer, no less lethal tone he added, "Here, call Jacques."

Had he been a betting man, Shafir would've put money on it that Garnier was not going to be pleased to hear from Megan. He considered the woman a menace.

She snatched the phone out of his hand, then hesitated.

"I don't know his number by rote—and you threw away my phone."

With a growl of impatience, Shafir took back his phone and located the number before handing it back.

Turning away from him, Megan bent over the backlit keypad before hitting the dial button.

"Jacques? Listen, I need your help."

There was silence. Every muscle in Shafir's body went taut as he waited.

After a long tense moment she thrust the phone at him and walked rapidly away. It appeared she really had believed that Garnier had been courting her. But that belief was clearly false and founded on a womanly need for love. Shafir watched her go, troubled by the notion that for Megan something priceless had just been destroyed.

In the breaking dawn Megan stood on the quaint balcony of her bedroom, her hands gripping the intricately carved railing as she stared blindly over the palace gardens as the first light from the east bathed them in a rosy glow.

How could she have gotten it so wrong?

Last night Jacques had been desperate to get off the phone and had told her never to call him again. It was obvious he'd answered only because he'd thought it was His Highness Prince Shafir al Dhahara calling, his fiancée's cousin. If he'd known it was her, she realized, he would've ignored her call.

As he must have ignored the message of distress she'd left for him days ago.

Despair filled her.

Oh, she'd come to Dhahara with such high hopes....

Jacques had seemed so right in every way. With his laughing green eyes and floppy hair, he was handsome in a dashing kind of way. He'd made her laugh...and his grand romantic gestures had threatened to sweep her off her feet. The bouquet of a hundred long-stemmed red roses, the huge box of Godiva chocolates, the crystal flagon of perfume. Sure, the sweet, drenching scent had been too overpowering, but she'd appreciated it. Only Jacques could have gotten away with such extravagant clichés. Somehow it made him even more endearing to her.

He'd made her feel so special.

So womanly and delicate, something that a female growing up with three brothers on a vineyard rarely felt. Femininity hadn't been a valued trait. Growing up, her brothers had preferred that she could ride and swim with them, and catch a cricket ball without dropping it, and survive an overzealous rugby tackle without dissolving into tears.

And, to be truthful, it wasn't just the over-the-top gifts, or even the fact that Jacques had seemed perfect. She'd been ready to fall headlong into love. Back home, her brothers had been falling like flies…looking starry-eyed and happy. And she'd wanted her turn, too.

Blowing out a hard breath, she admitted to herself that maybe she'd been in too much of a rush to love. Like an overripe peach, she'd been waiting for Jacques to come along and consume her.

Never again.

She'd reached that decision during the long hours of wakefulness through the night.

It was too humiliating.

She hadn't even realized that Jacques had been toying with her, though in hindsight all the signs had been there.

Sometimes his voice had lowered while they were talking. She'd thought it was sexy, but now she realized he hadn't wanted to be overheard. Not so sexy at all. The rat!

Often he hadn't been available to take her calls. She'd put that down to the fact that he was busy…a committed businessman, a wealthy high-profile entrepreneur. She'd been dazzled by his success, his suave good looks, his sexy talk.

How dumb could a woman get?

While she'd been hoping to find love, Jacques had been after a last fling before getting married. No wonder he hadn't been keen on her insistence on Dhahara as a holiday destination. No wonder he had wanted to stay as deep in the desert as possible.

Romance had nothing to do with it. He'd been leery of Zara's family uncovering the sordid truth.

They knew part of it. But thanks to Jacques they thought the worst of her. A gold digger, after a wealthy man.

How awful.

She heard a door close in the bedchamber behind her, and her hands tightened on the wooden railing. She didn't need to turn to know who had just entered her suite. And it wasn't Naema.

She didn't even wonder what he was doing here at this unspeakable time of the morning. She hadn't slept a wink last night—she'd been too upset, too ashamed by her bad judgment.

Stiffening, Megan waited for him to accuse her of further stupidity.

"See those palms?"

Relieved that she'd been granted a reprieve, Megan's eyes followed the path of his graceful hand to where a row of palms led to an arch set in a wall. Through the arch she glimpsed sunbeams reflecting off the surface of the largest pool, transforming it to a sheet of pure gold.

"I see them."

"They were planted by my father when he was a boy."

"King Selim planted them?" She knew she sounded disbelieving. "With his own hands?"

"He had some help, but he did a large part of the work himself."

Shafir moved up beside her and leaned forward to rest his elbows on the railing. The fresh scents of soap, sandalwood and that elusive spice were all too familiar. A sideways glance revealed that he wore a track suit, his feet bare and his hair damp. He must've come straight from a shower. The dawn light turned his skin to a warm bronze and added a sheen to his cheekbones. His amazing eyes were fiercely alive.

Megan looked away.

"My grandmother was a great believer in the power of gardens."

Tilting her face toward the rising sun, she said, "That's not surprising, given what you told me about your ancestor's Persian bride."

At the edge of her vision, she saw movement as Shafir nodded, and the bleak dull pain beneath her breast started to ease.

"She said the art of tending the gardens is a part of our heritage. She believed that they gave us spaces of stillness where we could reflect, that they brought great pleasure to life and that every child should experience the satisfaction of designing and building a piece of garden art."

She glanced at him again, a quick furtive look. "Did you build one?"

"Yes, a palmerie. It lies to the east of the palace."

"I haven't seen it."

"It's not part of the women's gardens."

The idea of that fierce segregation worried her. Her brows drew together. "So I'll never be allowed to see it then?"

"I will take you."

"You will?" She turned her head and stared at him in disbelief. Why would he grant her anything when he must despise her dreadfully. Damn Jacques!

"I will."

At his response, hope surged in her. "When?"

Perhaps time spent with him would give her a chance to show him the real Megan Saxon.

The side of his mouth kicked up. "You are always full of questions. What? Why? When? You need to learn patience."

For the first time since last night she felt her spirits lift. "Now you sound like my mother."

He looked intrigued. "Tell me about her."

"She's very elegant. Cultured. And she loves us all to death. The past year has been very hard for her—for all of us."

He didn't prompt her and Megan found herself wanting to tell him about it all. Perhaps then he might understand why she'd yearned for love and happiness.

"My brother died—Roland was killed in a car accident. Then we—that's me and my brothers Joshua and Heath— found out that my parents had adopted Roland before we were born."

"It was a shock?"

"Well, yes. It felt like a betrayal."

Shafir fell silent for a moment. In the distance the dark shapes of crows circled in the pale sky.

"I can understand that. I would have felt the same way."

"It was so hard to understand why they'd never told us. Mum said at first they thought we were all too young to deal with it, and later it became too hard to tell Roland. She was afraid it would've made him an outsider in his own family."

"I can understand that, too."

"But we loved him. It didn't matter that he was adopted. He was still our brother."

His hand closed over her fists where they clenched the railing. "Then you are fortunate to have shared his life for so many years."

The warmth from his fingers seeped into her skin.

"Yes, we were." What Shafir said was true. She was incredibly lucky to have grown up with Roland…and the rest of her tight-knit family. "But it was a difficult time. Before we'd had time to grieve for my brother, Rafaelo arrived."

"Rafaelo?" There was an odd note in his voice. "You met a man?"

Shafir lifted his hand away and she was conscious of a nagging sense of loss.

"No, no, nothing like that. Rafaelo is my father's illegitimate son, conceived not long after my parents adopted Roland. To make it worse, my mother knew nothing about his existence—or my father's affair. Nor did we."

He raised a dark, finely arched eyebrow. "That must have been another shock."

A breath of warm desert wind caught at her hair and Megan brushed the inky tendrils off her face. With a sense of shame she remembered the hostile reception they'd given Rafaelo. Megan was conscious of telling Shafir stuff she never shared. She wasn't normally given to confessing her life story to strangers. Yet oddly Shafir no longer seemed to be a stranger. And nor did she want him to continue to hold the impression that he already held. "I don't expect that you would understand how awful it was for us."

"Why shouldn't I?" His brows jerked together.

"Having half-brothers is a normal part of your society. There isn't the same expectation of fidelity of a married man."

"Only about seven percent of Dhaharans take a second wife." Shafir's bronze gaze was unrelenting. "But even then there is an expectation of honesty. Each wife knows where she stands in her husband's life. The number-one wife has more power than any other—and under Dhaharan law she must consent to her husband's taking a new wife before the wedding takes place, otherwise the marriage is void. And she would certainly know when one of her husband's other wives was pregnant."

"I would never agree to my husband marrying a second wife. I can't understand any woman putting herself in a position where such a thing might happen." Megan found such acceptance of a second wife impossible to understand.

Shafir lifted a shoulder and dropped it in a shrug. "The old ways are changing. Many modern Dhaharan women stipulate in a prenuptial agreement that their husband may not take another wife, and that they do not wish to reside with their in-laws. That is their right."

"They'd be silly not to do so." Megan considered him. "My mother thought she'd married Dad for better or worse, and she was shattered by the discovery of Dad's deception. For a while we all thought she was going to divorce him. She went to stay with her family. After a while she came back. Dad missed her terribly. And she forgave him."

Shafir held her gaze. "Your mother must love your father to forgive him. And if he loves her, he must regret his actions."

"He does! And he's doing everything he can to make it up to her." Megan couldn't bring herself to break the bond by looking away. A familiar frisson of awareness quivered through her. "But I could never forgive a man for that kind of betrayal. I hate Jacques."

It spilled out of her.

She clapped a hand over her mouth and drew a shuddering breath. "I didn't mean to say that. You're too easy to confide in."

He made a dismissive gesture with his hand. "I was taught to listen. And I never tell."

"Taught to listen?"

"It is part of our role as royalty. Every evening there

is *majlis*—people come from far and wide to tell us of their problems."

"I thought I knew him."

For a moment the abrupt change of subject confused Shafir. Then he realized Megan was talking about Jacques. He gave her a pitying look.

Her shoulders drooped. "I credited him with qualities he never had."

There was disillusionment in her voice and an air of dejection about her—the slump of her body, the hopelessness that flickered for a moment in her eyes. Shafir suppressed the first flare of doubt. Jacques couldn't have—would never have—double-crossed Zara. His fervent avowals of love aside, there was too much riding on the merger the wedding would bring—connections, increased wealth and trading opportunities. No man would risk such riches for an affair.

But having heard of her family's suffering, he couldn't help the wave of sympathy that swept him.

Averting his gaze from her, he stared over the desert, noticing that the group of crows had grown in size.

Did Megan still believe Jacques would be the man to make her forsake all others?

His gut tightened, and he came to a decision.

Swiveling on his heel, he placed his hands on her shoulders and drew her to face him. "I'm sorry."

Her eyes sparkled with the gloss of unshed tears. "Are you? Really sorry? I'm sorry," she parroted, "but I don't believe you."

Her bitterness knifed him. Shafir wanted to see the sparkle of joy back in her eyes. "I am very sorry that you feel you were deceived."

She made a sound of disgust. "I *was* deceived."

"I will accept that you didn't know Jacques was getting married."

"Gee, that's big of you."

He ignored that and continued, "But you read too much into a male business colleague's good manners, and you misinterpreted his intentions." Shafir gave a careless shrug. "It happens to men all the time."

Megan looked as though she was about to explode. Words appeared to fail her. Then he thought he heard the word *"arrogant"* and *"chauvinist"* but the rest disappeared in a hiss as her teeth snapped shut.

"We will agree to disagree about this," he said hastily.

"I suppose I misinterpreted the fact that you kidnapped me, too?" Megan glared at him, her hair gleaming as the sunlight danced across the black silk. "Is this the reason you abducted me? Because you thought that I knew about your cousin's wedding? Because you thought I'd come to Dhahara to stop it?"

What the devil was he supposed to say? He couldn't deny that. Shafir lifted his hand from her upper arm and cupped the soft skin of her cheek. "Megan, you must understand that—"

"Oh, I understand," Megan interrupted, her tone growing acid. "I understand that Jacques is a bastard."

Shafir blinked.

"As for you, Your Royal Highness, you're not much better." She slid out of his arms and sidled along the balcony.

"Hey, wait a minute—"

"You scared me nearly to death. Then you left me here to cool my heels—"

"In absolute luxury, with servants at your beck and call."

"I am not finished!"

Her back had straightened, and the dejection in her eyes had vanished. Fury and indignation came off her in waves, scorching Shafir.

"You never bothered to tell me what crime I'd been accused of. If I'd known what Jacques was like, I would've gladly left him for your cousin. Gift-wrapped, if she'd been dumb enough to still want him once she'd learned that he'd been two-timing both of us."

Shafir didn't bother to correct her that Jacques had done nothing wrong—the mistake had all been on her side.

Choosing his words carefully, he said, "I didn't tell you because in the beginning I didn't think it would make any difference." And once he'd taken her from the airport against her will, it had been too late to tell her—or to let her go. The papers would've been all over the story just as she'd threatened, and that would have wrecked the wedding anyway.

Tipping her head to one side, she scrutinized him through the slanting eyes that drove him wild. "Wouldn't make any difference? You thought that even if you told me, I wouldn't care? That I was after Jacques because he was rich? Because I'm the stereotypical little gold digger?"

His expression must've given him away, because she gave a derogatory laugh. "Now why doesn't that surprise me?"

"Megan—"

"You are rude, overbearing and incredibly arrogant. Do not interrupt me until I am finished," she warned as he started to protest. "You are every bit as much of a bastard as Jacques. You have no honor—"

That was too much. No one had ever dared make such accusations. Shafir descended on her. She continued to berate him, too far gone to realize that she'd gone past the boundaries that he would tolerate.

"Enough," he growled, his hands closing over her shoulders.

She was so soft. He eased his hold, but not his intent. Pulling her into his arms he slanted his mouth across hers, shutting off the tide of turbulent words.

He kissed her with hunger.

After a moment of stiff surprise, her lips softened and she kissed him back. She tasted sweet…so sweet.

She whimpered, a soft keening sound in the back of her throat.

Want overwhelmed him.

His hands trembled as they stroked along her back, finding the furrow of her spine under her wrap. He caressed the subtle valley, the firm flesh tempting him to touch more.

Silk bunched beneath his fingers as he cupped her buttocks and lifted her onto her tiptoes. The cradle of her hips rocked against his thighs, and desire exploded through him.

At last he lifted his head. "I should not have done that."

Shafir knew he should not be taking advantage of her while she was so vulnerable, so sure that she'd been betrayed by Garnier. But it was difficult to let her go, to step away from her and put the distance between them that his heart told him he needed to give her.

She was breathing fast, but the glazed look vanished quickly. "You're right. You should not."

Her tongue tip flicked over her bottom lip, moistening the soft pad of flesh.

He groaned at the provocative gesture. "How am I supposed to resist you?"

Lifting her easily, he strode through the doors off the balcony into the bedchamber, to the ancient, carved bed. He let her slide slowly down his body, aware of every delectable inch of her womanly body.

But instead of subsiding onto the bed behind her, Megan struggled out of his arms. "No, I don't want this. I don't even want to be here."

"After kissing me like you'd discovered paradise, where else would you like to be?"

"I want to go home."

* * *

"You want me to take you back to Jacques?" Shafir shook his head as if to clear it of confusion. "Even though you believe he two-timed you and know he is about to marry another woman?"

Megan stared at him in disappointment. Clearly he'd thought by kissing her he'd silence her into submission. No chance.

"If I never see bloody Jacques again this side of eternity, that would be too soon." She brushed her hair back from her face with shaking hands.

"Then…" He took a step forward.

Dropping her hands, she scrambled away from him. "Stay away from me!"

She didn't want him kissing her again. Despite her bravado, she had to admit his kisses caused her head to spin. And they made her crave all sorts of things she'd never considered—how much she wanted to kiss him and see where it would lead. How could she have mistaken the liking she felt for Jacques for passion? And how could any man, however courtly, ever be more desirable than this savage sheik?

Ah, hell.

"I never want to see you again, either. Or anyone else from this blighted country." She flung the words at him from the opposite side of the four-poster bed to prevent herself from caving in and letting him take her all the way to paradise. "I want to go home."

Edging around the giant bed, she glanced desperately toward the door.

And in case there should be any further misunderstanding, she held his gaze and said as firmly as she could manage, "I want to go home to New Zealand, back to my family."

Shafir didn't react. He just stood there looking unmoved by her plea.

She drew a ragged breath. "No need to worry that I'm a threat to Jacques's wedding to your cousin. I don't want him." But to her horror he was already shaking his head. "You can't refuse!"

"You can't go home yet."

Tears of frustration and thwarted rage thickened her throat. In a tight, hoarse voice, she said, "*Why?* You have no reason to imprison me any longer."

"Oh, yes, I do."

"What do you mean?"

"If I let you go home, you will tell your family that you were kidnapped—"

"So?" He was dreaming if he thought she was going to agree to say nothing. "Last time I heard, freedom of speech still existed—or doesn't Dhahara go in for that?"

"My country is very enlightened."

Megan couldn't help herself—she laughed. All the empathy she'd felt with him not so long ago evaporated. He was back to being the hard-assed, arrogant jerk she hated. "Sure," she scoffed. "And you're a very liberated man."

"It is for this reason that I cannot let you go."

Megan laughed more loudly and hoped he didn't hear the edge of hysteria that underpinned it. "Because I have a great sense of humor? Or because I'm not afraid to stand up and tell you what you are? A kidnapper, a thief and a liar."

She heard the breath he sucked in.

Good! Let him count to ten for a change.

"Because you have a sister-in-law who is a journalist."

"You should have thought of the likely fallout that would happen before kidnapping me. People deserve to know what you did. You might be a member of the royal family, you might control the tourism ministry in Dhahara, but your actions are inexcusable." Immediately after her outburst Megan wished, for once in her life, that she'd kept her overzealous mouth shut. Why, oh, why had she allowed him to push her buttons? Now he had even less reason to let her go.

For the first time in days apprehension quaked through her. She was in a remote region, far from help, and under his absolute control. She'd convinced herself he wasn't going to hurt her…but when would he let her go? Or did he plan to keep her incarcerated indefinitely?

At last she voiced her fear. "What if I promise never to say anything? Then will you release me?"

"Yes, I will let you go—after the wedding."

Relief surged through her. He didn't intend to lock her up and throw away the key. Then caution kicked in. "How long away is that?"

"Two weeks."

"Two weeks?"

Her relief evaporated. Right now fourteen days of living in proximity with Shafir seemed like a life sentence. In the bright morning light she scanned his face. The chinks of bronze, the bladed nose and the chiseled mouth that had not so long ago kissed her with such passion. She dared not let herself even think about that.

She couldn't stay. He was too dangerous to her peace of mind. "Please Shafir, let me go."

He shook his head, his eyes filled with an emotion akin to regret. "Not until Zara is married. Nothing is going to derail the wedding."

A wave of frustration swept through her at his utter intransigence. She wished she had the courage to yell at him and beat her fists against the wall of his chest. Instead she said, "I can't believe you'd let a rat like Jacques marry the cousin you must dearly love."

Seven

I can't believe you'd let a rat like Jacques marry the cousin you must dearly love.

Megan's parting words nagged at the edges of Shafir's mind as he strode through the palmerie he'd planted years ago. He told himself they were the angry words of an angry woman who believed she'd been scorned. The words held no truth. Right now Megan was intent on getting back at Jacques.

She'd do whatever she could to convince Shafir to call off the wedding.

And Shafir had no intention of being manipulated just because of a kiss that had offered him a glimpse of heaven.

He stopped abruptly, staring unseeingly at palm trees and rocks that had been landscaped to look wild and natural. Yet he couldn't forget the feel of her skin under the filmy wrap she'd worn, or the curves of her body as she'd arched against him....

He shook off the memory.

It had been over too damn quickly.

But it wouldn't change his mind. Megan had misread her business relationship with Jacques and misconstrued his courtesy. Zara and Jacques would get married as planned. It would be a good union, with benefits to both families, and leading to improved trade opportunities for the Garnier corporation and increased distribution channels for Dhahara's exports. Being a Garnier would catapult Zara into the top echelons of European society, a world where she would thrive.

He certainly wasn't about to be swayed by a lush, womanly body—or even by a bewildered expression and a pair of hurt eyes.

Yet Shafir couldn't deny that Megan's desperation to go home made him feel curiously guilty. Her unhappiness was a marked contrast to the sexy, seductive woman who had welcomed him back from Katar. And, despite now knowing that the flirtatious looks and soft touches had all been an act aimed at putting him in an uncomfortable position with his imagined fiancée, he was male enough to want that desirable woman back.

He tipped his head back and stared at the clear blue sky.

Nor did he like the notion that Megan viewed him with the same contempt and dislike that she now felt toward Jacques. She'd branded them both with the same harsh label. He didn't care for that at all.

And Dhahara didn't deserve to be dismissed as a blighted country.

He was sure that once Megan had a chance to reflect, she would realize that she'd been unfair to Jacques. But he suspected he'd have to work harder to change her low opinion of himself. She considered him a thief and a kidnapper. It would take some work to convince her he was not the ruthless bastard she believed him to be. And that Dhahara was the most special place in the world.

And he had only fourteen days in which to change her mind.

"There is another reason I can't let you go," Shafir told Megan later that day when they encountered each other in the small salon.

Still enraged by his assumption that she'd misread Jacques's very clear intentions, Megan had retreated inside to get out of the sweltering late afternoon heat and had been hoping for a quiet cup of mint tea to help her calm down. Now she hesitated on the threshold at the sight of Shafir ensconced in an armchair reading a newspaper.

"Oh, and why is that?" She'd successfully avoided him all day. Now she entered the room with reluctance.

"I want to change your mind."

Megan raised her eyebrows. "You think you can change my opinion about you?"

Folding the newspaper and dropping it on the floor beside him, Shafir said, "I don't care that you think I'm a bastard, a thief or a liar."

Yet Megan noticed that his fist curled into his lap. Clearly her opinion had rankled.

"But I want the chance to give you a better impression of Dhahara, of its people," he continued.

So he hadn't appreciated her dismissal, her reference to his homeland as a blighted place.

"I don't think you can." She perched herself on the edge of the sofa nearest the door, the better to make a quick escape. "The perceptions I have of Dhahara are not good. It would take dynamite to change them."

"But you love the palace and gardens."

"That's true," she conceded. "And the stories you told me about your ancestors were fascinating, too."

"It's not all the people of Dhahara you detest—you're fond of Aniya and Naema. I've seen the way you talk to them."

"That is true, too." She drew a deep breath. "You know, it's weird. I really wanted to visit Dhahara. Ever since I first heard that Jacques had business with the kingdom I've been fascinated. Coming here was a supposed to be the fulfilment of a fantasy."

"It can still be," said Shafir.

But Megan was shaking her head. "It's too late. I'm no longer the same person I was when I arrived in Dhahara. I've given up on the fantasy."

Stretching folded arms above his head, Shafir admired the picture she made with her dark hair and eyes against the deep red sofa before saying, "So you still believe this nonsense that Jacques was trying to seduce you?"

Her chin came up a notch. "It's not nonsense. And I never said he was trying to seduce me—he convinced me that it was possible for us to fall in love with each other."

Shafir clicked his tongue dismissively. "Women fall in love at the inflection of a man's voice, at the sight of a handsome face."

"Not me."

Something tightened in Shafir's chest at the idea of Megan falling for Jacques. "So you can prove this?"

"Prove it?" Megan's puzzled gaze met his.

Shafir forced himself not to be drawn into the dark, sultry depths. "Prove that Jacques was pursuing you."

She leaned forward. "Oh, yes. He sent me roses and chocolate. And there's the fact that I wanted to stay in a hotel in the medina of Katar—but Jacques thought the desert might be more romantic."

"Jacques made accommodation bookings?"

Megan slowly shook her head. "No, I did. I booked a night in Katar and for the rest of my time here I booked a remote villa in the desert." She made a sound of disgust. "Obviously Jacques was afraid of being seen with me in the capital."

Shafir ignored the last. "The chocolates and flowers are gone, and Jacques never made the booking. So you have no proof of these things you accuse Jacques of?"

"There was my cell phone—I'd kept the texts he'd sent. But, of course, you got rid of that."

"How convenient for you."

Her eyes took on a militant glint. "Are you accusing me of lying? Of making up stories about Jacques? Why would I do that?"

He considered that. Then dismissed it. He was quite sure that Megan wasn't a liar. But she was a woman. And women were prone to flights of fancy—especially where love was concerned. Perhaps Jacques had sent her flowers and chocolates. Nothing wrong with that. Why, he's sent those to staff and colleagues, too. In appreciation. Or as a marketing strategy. In which case, Megan had misconstrued a gesture that meant nothing more than "Thank you." "You told me yourself you came to Dhahara seeking adventure, excitement and romance."

"Because of Jacques."

Impatience rose in him. Clearly she was still determined to make Jacques out to be a villain. The truth of the matter was that she had simply misconstrued Jacques's behavior as a result of a typically feminine desire to be loved.

"Jacques was nothing more than a work colleague. The romance is all in your own mind. There's not a shred of evidence that Jacques did anything wrong."

* * *

"There is something I want to show you today, Megan."

They had finished breakfast. Megan had eaten in silence, not once lifting her eyes to meet his. Knowing it was her way of conveying her displeasure, Shafir remained unruffled. The day was clear, promising to be dry and hot. He rose to his feet, impatient to be gone before the real heat set in. "Put on something comfortable—sweats or jeans."

Megan remained seated, but her lashes flicked up to reveal expressionless eyes. "Is this part of your campaign to change my mind about Dhahara?"

He only smiled.

Although Shafir had claimed he didn't care what she thought about him, he knew he did. Now he examined the short-sleeved T-shirt she wore. "Don't forget to wear a long-sleeved shirt for the sun." He didn't want that exquisite creamy skin burned.

Finally she pushed back her chair and asked, "Where are we going?"

At least she hadn't refused to come. "You will see."

When he met Megan at the door to the courtyard twenty minutes later, jeans peeked out from under the loose abaya he'd sent up, and he could see the collar of a white shirt at her neckline and white cuffs jutting out where the robe fell back to expose her lower arms.

"Are we going riding?" she asked.

"There's a village not far from here, with an *ain*. A spring," he clarified. "I thought you might enjoy a camel ride."

Excitement lit up her face. "A camel ride. That would be—" The excitement dimmed as she broke off.

She was still angry at him for speaking the truth yesterday, Shafir realized.

But she would come around. Sooner or later she would have to admit that he was right.

* * *

The *ain* was surrounded by clumps of leafy tamarisk and carob trees that guarded the entrance to the village. The scent of wild mint filled the air as the camels lumbered under the branches. After being exposed to the hot sun in the desert, Megan found the cool greenness a welcome relief.

Ahead, Shafir pulled his camel to a halt and Megan came up beside him.

"Legend has it that this is where my ancestor brought his Farrin to drink from the healing water of this spring. The village is named *Ain Farrin* after the spring and his Persian bride."

Megan forgot that she'd meant to be silent and reserved to remind Shafir of her ire at his arrogant dismissal of her grievances against Jacques. Bursting into speech, she asked, "Did they build the well, too?" She pointed to the stone structure that looked like it had stood there for a long time.

He shook his head. "That is the labor of later generations. It still operates."

He'd barely finished when a gaggle of children came running, drawn like magnets to the visitors. Shafir grinned and waved. The group grew bigger and louder as they proceeded into the heart of the village. Megan couldn't help thinking they must look like a Pied Piper procession.

She was laughing by the time the camels sank down and they finally dismounted.

Several of men came to embrace Shafir, and back-slappings and greetings were exchanged. He drew Megan forward and the babble subsided. "Come," he said, "Ahmed and Mona have invited us to their home for a cup of coffee."

He led her to where a couple waited.

Deep laugh lines were carved into Ahmed's face under the checked black-and-white *ghutrah* he wore on his head.

He gently drew the woman who had been waiting beside him forward. "This is my wife, Mona."

There was pride in his voice, and Mona gave him a secret little smile that revealed their love without a word.

Their home was a simple dwelling constructed of blocks of stone and baked earth. Inside, it was spotless. The kitchen was dominated by an open-fire oven set in one wall. There were several trays of dough already in the oven and the warm smell of baking filled the room.

Megan was soon sipping *gahwa,* the strong bitter coffee that left a tang in her mouth. Mona produced triangles of baklava that melted on her tongue. Ahmed had cornered Shafir and the two men sat with their heads together, as Ahmed fired off what was clearly a string of questions.

"I'm sorry," Mona said to Megan. "My husband is rude talking in our language. But he can't resist the chance to get the sheik's view on the new school we are building."

Not for the first time Megan wished she could speak a smattering of Arabic, and she mentioned that to Mona. Mona instantly offered to teach her what she could, and the next half hour passed in gales of laughter that drew smiles of indulgence from both men.

A young girl carrying a tray with balls of dough entered the house and Mona took the tray from her, exchanging a few words in Arabic. And this time Megan understood a few of the pleasantries and thank-yous that followed.

"Ahmed is the village baker," Shafir murmured to Megan as they departed. "People bring the breads they have prepared and he bakes them."

"Oh."

"I'm sorry that I left you to your own devices."

She gave him a smile and watched as his concern for her eased from his eyes. "No need to apologize, Mona is very sweet, and I understand that Ahmed wanted your advice on a matter that is important to the community."

Shafir hoped that the day had given Megan fresh insight into Dhahara. On the ride back, her face was thoughtful, and, despite that fact that she must be sore from the camel's uncomfortable gait, she made no complaint. The coolness that she'd exhibited at the start of the day had evaporated, and he was glad. He resolved not to be drawn into any discussions about Jacques; it only created unpleasant tension between them.

Back at the palace they dismounted and Megan stroked the nose of her camel.

"Thank you."

The camel harrumphed.

Shafir couldn't help it—he laughed at the expression on her face.

Megan glanced over and poked a pink tongue out at him. "The nose is so soft. Like velvet." She stroked again and Shafir felt his smile start to slip. He wished her hands were stroking him like that.

"Did you enjoy the ride?" he asked abruptly.

"Oh, yes." Her face lit up. "I loved the desert...it's so wide and open. I've never felt anything like it. The *ain* was such a contrast, so cool and green. And Mona and Ahmed were so welcoming."

Shafir hesitated. "I heard you tell Mona that you would like to learn to speak Arabic. Is that true?"

She frowned at him. "Of course it was true. Why should I lie about something like that?"

"Perhaps you were being polite."

She fell silent. Then she said, "I want to learn. It's frustrating not being able to follow the conversation around me."

"It won't be easy," he warned.

"I know." She lifted her chin. "But I think I'll catch on quickly. I speak tolerable French and I found that easy to learn."

Jacques. A flare of emotion dangerously akin to envy spread through Shafir. Had she learned to speak French to impress her business connection?

"Arabic is not French," he growled, relinquishing the reins of his camel to a groom and following her up the stairs that led to the palace. "It is far more complex and has nuances it can take years to understand."

She stopped at the top of the stairway. "Hey, I don't intend to get a doctorate in the language. I only want to gain some insight into the people and the land during the time that I am here."

He pounced on that. "So you will not fight me with demands to go home?"

There was astonishment as her eyes met his. "Yes, I want to stay. I had a wonderful day. I hope that the next thirteen days will be as good."

Pleasure warmed Shafir. "I am pleased," he said simply.

"That's what you intended, wasn't it?" Awareness dawned in her slanted eyes. "You're incredibly sneaky." But she was smiling and there was no barb to the words.

Shafir grinned back. "I will have to make sure that every day is better than the day before. You are generous to give Dhahara a chance." But what he really meant was that she'd given him another chance. A chance to prove he wasn't the criminal jerk she considered him to be.

"Put like that, how can I possibly refuse? If I do, I lose the quality of generosity."

"If you leave and go home you will never know what you missed out on."

A shadow crossed her face. "I've already missed out on what I came for."

She was talking about romance...excitement... adventure. His gut tightened. "Sometimes what you think you want is not what you really need," he said enigmatically.

"That sounds like a riddle."

"Perhaps it is." To him Megan was the most complex riddle of them all. One that he was trying his best to figure out and understand. Not once today had she shown any flighty feminine traits. Not once had she misconstrued anything anyone had said. So why had she been so desperate to fall for Jacques?

The next few days passed in a whirl of activity. Megan had to admit that Shafir was doing a marvelous job at showing her a side of Dhahara she would never have discovered on her own and making sure that each day surpassed the one before.

As long as she didn't discuss Jacques and stayed away from contentious topics like Jacques chasing her while he was engaged to Zara—which Shafir simply refused to accept—or her belief that Shafir should put a stop to the wedding, they got along just fine.

For a royal prince, he'd proved to be an enthusiastic guide. Penance, she decided. He was doing penance for the wrong he'd done by bringing her here against her will.

The souk they'd visited that day had been an eye-opener. Located at the crossroads of two ancient desert routes, the stalls had been crammed together and people seemed to have come from all corners of the earth to sell their goods. There were caftans, carpets, baskets, jewelry and even goats for sale.

From the instant she'd stepped out of the vehicle, Megan was astounded by the explosion of color. Red. Turquoise.

Gold. Ochre. While the backdrop of the bleached gold of the desert made her reach for her sunglasses.

Then she became aware of the babble of noise. Slowly it separated into discernable sounds. The croaking of three black crows perched on a railing nearby. The *mah-mah* of goats bleating. Vendors chanting to attract buyers.

There were big bins full of spices. A jumble of rugs, copper pots, porcelain and fabrics in all the colors of the rainbow filled the stalls.

Megan hurried forward and touched the brightly hued silks with reverent fingers. "These are beautiful," she murmured as Shafir came up behind her.

A merchant appeared from nowhere and almost bowed to the ground when he recognized his illustrious visitor.

"Look at this." She drew a bolt of deep-pink silk off the rail. "The color, it's amazing."

She held it up against herself. A breath of mischievous wind blew off the headscarf she'd tied in a makeshift *hijab* around her hair.

Shafir's breath caught in his throat.

"It suits you." Against her windswept dark hair and pale skin the color glowed like a rich jewel, throwing her coloring into sharp relief. With the slope of her eyes, she looked exotic. Beautiful. Infinitely desirable. Shafir felt heat stir in his groin.

"We will take it." He shot a glance at the merchant, knowing it was folly to announce his intention before the barter started. But to his surprise the merchant was shaking his head.

"A gift. It is an honor to supply a garment for your lady."

Megan cast a quick glance at Shafir before turning to bestow a dazzling smile on the merchant. "Thank you. I'll treasure it always."

"The pleasure belongs to me." The merchant bowed to Shafir. "You have chosen well, Your Highness."

Shafir wanted to explain. Then he decided it was better to keep silent. News traveled with the speed of a sandstorm in the desert. Yet right now he couldn't even define their relationship himself, and he certainly didn't want the entire population of Dhahara speculating about it.

"I want to buy some things for my brothers...my sisters-in-law." Her face alight, she darted in and out between the stalls, her enthusiasm boundless.

Shafir didn't need to warn her about paying unrealistic prices. It was clear that she knew exactly what the items she selected were worth—and how much she was prepared to pay for the fabrics and jewelry she bought.

He stood by, conscious of the smiles she attracted—and the curious glances cast in his direction. He cursed himself for not giving a thought to how she might stand out here, how memorable she might be.

"Oh, look, Shafir."

He turned his head to see what had drawn her attention. A camel was tied to a post near where the trio of crows had settled earlier.

"Isn't he sweet?"

"Be careful." He hastened to warn her. "Camels can be exceedingly bad-tempered."

"Not this one. Are you, my sweetie?" she crooned in a tone that sent vibrations down Shafir's spine.

"You don't need a camel."

"I wish I could take him home. But how could I put you in my luggage, gorgeous?" She glanced up. "What about you, Shafir? Couldn't you use another?"

"I have sufficient camels."

"That camel is already sold, but I have another madam might like."

Megan started as the wizened camel trader appeared. "Oh, I'm sorry. I hope you don't mind me patting him." She apologized and threw him a smile that had Shafir gnashing his teeth. Why couldn't she smile at him with that carefree joy?

He resisted the impulse to tell her to cover up. Except for her loose hair, she was already quite respectable. It wasn't her fault that her smile, her *joie de vivre,* drew attention—it had attracted him from the first, too.

As he watched Megan charm the weary camel trader, Shafir decided Jacques must be made of steel to have resisted the temptation Megan offered. Idly he wondered how Jacques had failed to notice that Megan was building hopes of a romance around their business meetings. Why had Jacques not put a stop to it? Had he been flattered?

Brooding now, Shafir decided he needed to have a word with the man and warn him to tone down his Gallic charm so that there could be no more misunderstandings.

But the unease that had settled in the pit of his stomach would not relent. Still watching Megan chatting, Shafir cast his mind over the time he'd spent with Megan during the past days—and could remember no hint of flirtatious behavior.

Not even with him. And he found himself missing the seductive smiles and soft touches that had clearly been nothing more than a ploy to punish him for kidnapping her. It had worked—it had made him sweat.

Yet Megan had not followed up on her advantage.

Shafir knew he was extremely eligible. If it had been a wealthy man Megan was after, she would have wasted no time pursuing him. But she hadn't.

Instead they'd spent evenings listening to music together and the days out exploring—and talking about everything under the sun. Except the tense triangle between Megan, Jacques and Zara.

And every hour in her company had confirmed that Megan was funny and smart.

Now she was laughing at something the camel trader had

said. The man smiled, too, a gummy grin where he no longer possessed teeth. He heard her try out an Arabic phrase, saw the surprised pleasure that lit the trader's face.

What if Megan had not been misguided? What if Jacques had flirted with her, romanced her and had deliberately led her to believe he was falling in love with her?

Shafir didn't want to believe it. If that was true then he couldn't possibly allow Zara to marry Jacques. And he'd have to break the awkward news to Zara that Jacques had been two-timing her. He shuddered at the thought of bringing pain to a young woman he had protected from hardship since she was a child.

It was the thought of Zara's pain that gave him pause. Although there wasn't a lot of time left before the wedding, he had no intention of acting recklessly or breaking Zara's heart unless he was very certain.

He'd take a few days to consider carefully what needed to be done. And the place he thought most clearly was in the empty space of the desert.

Making the decision gave him a sense of relief. They would leave in the morning.

"Your woman is like fire. She crackles with energy."

Shafir bit back the retort that Megan was not his woman. He turned from where he was busy filling his horse's saddle bag with provisions for the return trip to Qasr Al-Ward to see what the *Bedu* elder, who had come quietly up behind him, was referring to.

He discovered Megan surrounded by a group of women and children and, in typical Megan fashion, he could see that she was talking, using a scattering of Arabic words and waving her hands in the air to help convey her meaning. Her wide smile flashed as one of the other women said something.

Shafir felt himself start to smile, too.

It was easy to see why the tribal elder compared her to leaping flames.

"Yes," he agreed. "And like a fire, she warms everyone around her." It was true, he realized. His life had changed since the day he'd taken Megan from the airport. Every day seemed brighter, filled with more. His staff were fond of her, and here at a Bedouin camp in the desert, again she charmed people.

"She will always be of fire—do not seek to change her, Prince Shafir."

The old tribesman's words were cryptic. Last night Megan had sat with the same group of women beside the great communal fire while men clad in pristine white robes performed dances with sticks. Her face had reflected excitement and pleasure, and Shafir had wondered if this was the adventure that she had sought by coming to Dhahara.

"Like fire, she has strength," he replied. "I do not think the man has been born who can change her."

"You are wise not to want to change such a woman. Bring her to visit us again. She will be welcomed."

"I will." Shafir moved away from the saddlebags to embrace the old man.

"Prince Shafir," the elder tapped Shafir's arm. "Remember to dance with the flame, too. You are still young for the burdens that have been placed on your shoulders. You must remember to enjoy yourself—to laugh sometimes."

Shafir inclined his head.

For the first time in his life the desert had brought him no peace—and he was no nearer to a decision than when they'd arrived. Was it any wonder he didn't feel like laughing?

As he went to tell Megan that it was almost time to leave, he knew that the choice he had to make was simple: to tell Zara it was possible that Jacques had not been faithful, or to remain silent and let the wedding proceed because, as yet, he had no proof. It was only that his unease had grown with every day he got to know Megan better, until he was prepared to admit that she probably had not been mistaken. His gaze lingered on her, and she looked up and threw him a quick smile that lit up her eyes and caused his heart to contract in his chest. Then a toddler tugged at her skirt and she glanced away. The moment of connection was past.

Megan wasn't flighty or flirty or any of the other ridiculous things women could be.

But it wasn't his life that would lie in tatters if Megan was proved right. It would be Zara's life that would be shattered.

The only other course of action was to confront Jacques. But if the Frenchman had been mucking around, he was hardly going to admit it.

Shafir knew that speaking to his father and brothers would bring him no closer to a solution. They'd all believed that Megan was here in Dhahara to force Zara and Jacques apart. No one was going to believe her without proof.

Except perhaps him.

Eight

It was four days after they had set off into the desert. They were riding the same stocky horses along the same route through a craggy wadi when danger struck.

Over the course of the days spent at the Bedouin encampment, Megan had come to realize that Shafir was wildly popular out here in the desert—that everyone knew him. He listened to the goatherd's father's complaint that his son was missing too much of the village school, laughed at the village elders' observation that it was time for him to get married and agreed to an old woman's request for a new loom.

He listened. And more than that, he cared.

The man she'd thought little more than a savage was turning out to have depths that she would never have guessed. Megan was still musing about how wrong she'd been in her initial estimation of Shafir's character when Hanif came riding hard across the desert and spoke to Shafir in a volley of Arabic.

Megan turned her head.

One glance showed her all she needed to know. Bandits. Red headscarfs wound around their heads, faces covered in black beards, scruffy ponies.

"Oh, no."

"Don't worry." Shafir rode closer to her.

"But they don't look like Dhaharans."

"Some might be. And the rest will come from Marulla, which lies behind the mountain ranges. There is no oil in their country…infighting amongst their sheiks and the ravages of war on their far border have taken their toll."

The group kept coming toward them.

Shafir wheeled his horse around.

"Stay here," he commanded. "Hanif, take care of her."

He rode forward.

Megan watched him go, feeling helpless. How could she ever have suspected him of being a bandit? The difference was marked. He sat proud in the saddle, centuries of Dhaharan pride showing.

The untamed one. What a catch a royal prince would be for this ragged group.

This time the dangers of kidnap and ransom were not aimed at her, but at Shafir.

The fool!

Why had he put himself at risk?

The scrape of metal caught her attention. A sideways glance revealed that the guard now riding beside her held a rifle low across his leg, out of sight to the approaching riders.

The other guard had moved up behind Shafir's mount. For the first time she realized that their escort was heavily armed. No doubt Shafir carried a weapon in the bag strapped across the front of his saddle, too. For all his fierceness, the aura of raw power that he carried with him, Shafir was not reckless.

He was no fool, this desert prince.

But she did not want to see him hurt.

Strangely she gave no thought to her own safety, about what might happen if these rough men captured her. All her thoughts were of him. He was the person of consequence, and he would be the greatest prize.

She urged her horse forward.

"Madam," Hanif spoke, "don't go. You will only distract His Highness from the task at hand."

"But he is in danger."

Hanif gave her a sun-beaten smile. "Not today. He will be fine. Wait and you will see. Insha'allah."

The inevitability of it all made her want to scream. Instead she reined back the mare and watched as Shafir raised a hand and called out a greeting. Two men from the other group trotted out. The three horses and their riders stood bunched together, Shafir's guard hanging back.

Anxiety filled her. "Why's he letting them get so close?"

"They are talking to him," said Hanif peaceably.

"I can see that," she snapped, growing edgier by the minute.

"They have a problem."

She stared at the older man with suspicion. "How do you know that? Do you know these men?"

He lost his air of insouciance. "I would never lead His Highness into an ambush. I have been with him since he was a boy." He pointed. "But if you look, you will see that he is listening. These men are men with something weighing on their minds. The sheik will fix it. It is what he does best."

Megan followed the line of the bent finger. Shafir's head was tilted to one side—as it had been when she'd told him about her brother's death. Even as she watched, he gave that slight nod, that small incline of his head that she'd come to know so well.

He was not going to be abducted…or worse, killed.

She would have another chance to meet those bronze eyes, to touch him, to talk to him.

Megan didn't want to put a name to the emotions that careened through her when he finally swung his horse away from the other men and rode back to where she and Hanif waited.

But she knew that she would never again believe that she hated him.

Megan stepped onto the top step of the largest pool in the Garden of Pools and the silken water rippled around her legs. Slowly she lowered herself into the deliciously soothing water that sparkled in the slanting light of the sinking sun.

Despite the fright the encounter with the bandits had given her, Megan still couldn't bring herself to regret the trip into the desert, which had shown her a different side of the man who aroused such complex emotions within her.

Shafir had kept her safe.

Her fear for him earlier had been very real. She'd *cared* about what might happen to him out in the sun-bleached desert. She'd been terrified that something might happen to him.

And it wasn't a fear for herself.

It was all for him.

Crazily, somehow he'd started to become important to her.

Stockholm syndrome, she thought cynically. The captive starting to become dependent on the captor.

Diving deep into the still water to escape the disturbing notion, she stroked for the other side of the pool, the cerulean blue and ochre patterns of the mosaics vivid beneath her. Ten minutes later, lungs bursting from plowing up and down, Megan exploded to the surface, only to find the man who had hijacked her thoughts sitting on the edge of a lounger, a towel wrapped around his waist as he toed off a pair of docksiders.

She stood, uncertain of protocol when she was so scantily dressed in only a bikini. She'd always been alone at the pools, with only Naema coming to see if she required anything. Should she leave?

"I won't be long."

"Take your time. There's enough space for both of us." He rose to his full height and loosened the towel.

Megan caught a glimpse of a narrow black Speedo, narrow hips and wide muscled shoulders turned bronze by the sun, before she whipped her eyes away and sank back under the water to where the patterned mosaics created an exotic underwater world.

There was a dull splash behind her. She swam faster. She wasn't ready to confront what she felt about him.

Not yet.

A moment later the water beside her moved and she knew Shafir had caught up with her.

She closed her eyes and waited for a surge of water to tell her he had passed. But he stayed with her. Opening her eyes, she lifted her head and took a breath. His strokes were lazy, just enough to keep up with her. When she reached the other end she grabbed the side and trod water.

He stopped, too.

"Go ahead," she said. "Do your laps, I don't need entertaining."

His eyes crinkled and the sides of his mouth curled up. "Maybe I do."

Her heart stopped at the impact of his smile. He'd been so serious over the past few days—somber, almost reserved. She'd forgotten the *wow* feeling when he beamed that full wattage at her.

Megan scrambled to collect her thoughts and find her

voice. Play it cool. No need for him to know about the turmoil churning inside her. "Uh…so now I'm entertainment, am I?"

"I like watching you."

What the hell was that supposed to mean? Was it a line? "Really?"

He nodded. "Really. You have an amazingly expressive face."

Oh, no. She rolled her eyes and hoped he didn't see what a mess she was in. "Not that again!"

"What do you mean?"

"That's what my family says. My mother says, when I was a little girl, she could tell with one look whether I was lying to her. And I'm always in trouble for putting my foot in it." She laughed, lightly, almost convincing herself that her world hadn't turned upside down out there in the desert today when she'd thought she might lose him to a bunch of bandits. Glancing away from his piercing gaze, she said with deliberate irony, "I can't keep a secret to save my life."

"Well, then, I know never to tell you my secrets."

"You have secrets?"

"Plenty," he said in a husky voice that made her tingle. "If-I-tell-you-then-I'll-have-to-kill-you kind of secrets?"

He burst into laughter. "That's why you entertain me."

"Thanks. I think."

He drifted closer.

"It's a pleasure." There was definitely a light in his eyes now.

"Are you flirting with me?" The words erupted before she'd thought about them, and Megan found herself blushing furiously. "Sorry, ignore that, I shouldn't have said it. Of course you're not flirting with me."

"You want to know my intentions?" His eyes were half closed, concealing the fierce predatory eyes.

"Yes," she said boldly.

"I don't know." He looked surprised at the admission. After a beat, he said, "Maybe I am flirting with you."

Well, the man had faced possible death today. Hardly surprising he was doing things he would normally never contemplate.

He drifted closer still and his legs brushed hers. A bolt of electricity surged through Megan followed by a rush of excitement.

"That's entertainment, right?" There should have been a slight snap to the comment, instead it came out breathless.

"This is entertainment."

He kissed her. His mouth sleek and knowing and very, very experienced.

Megan didn't find it entertaining. It was overwhelming, scary. Anything but entertaining.

When it ended she almost said "wow." But she managed to bite it back. She wasn't going to let him know how much the kiss had shaken her.

So she decided to amuse him—she might as well give him the entertainment he sought. "If you kiss me, do you have to kill me?"

He didn't laugh. Instead he looked offended. "What kind of man do you think I am? An animal?"

She stared into those bronze eyes, thought about the power in his shoulders, the wild grace with which he moved.

"Well?" He was frowning now.

"You're not an animal."

"That—" his gaze scanned her face "—was not convincing."

She was conscious of how close he was, of how little clothes they wore. And against all odds a frisson of excitement shivered through her.

"Well, you're hardly a pussycat." She dropped her

lashes, reluctant for him to read the strange awareness that was pulsing through her, tightening her skin and the tips of her breasts. Signs she was sure he would read without hesitation.

"A pussycat? What kind of man wants to be a pussycat?" He sounded disgusted.

Megan glanced up, and their gazes meshed.

"Megan!"

Her name was a hoarse groan. And she knew that he'd seen exactly how she felt.

This time he trapped her against the wall, the full length of his body plastered against hers. Shafir's mouth opened on hers, ravenous, demanding. And she gave him everything he wanted.

When the kiss ended, her breath was coming in shallow pants. "You could've been killed today."

She could have bitten her tongue out the moment the words escaped.

"But I wasn't."

His legs brushed hers under the water and she felt his arousal. Passion and fury surged through her. "It was stupid to ride out to meet them."

"I recognized one of them…he is the son of a cousin of Ahmed's neighbor. His family worries about him. I told him I will carry news back to them about him. He knows I couldn't do that if they killed me. And the men wanted my help. I can't help them if I'm dead."

It sounded so reasonable, almost prosaic, but it did nothing to soothe the terrible cold fear that still lingered in the aftermath.

"You were worried about me."

There was an intensity in the fierce eyes.

Her eyelashes fell. "No."

He put a finger under her chin and lifted it. "Yes."

She met his eyes in the waning light and found herself searching them frantically. Earlier there'd been that awful moment when she'd wondered if she'd ever have the chance to do this again. Or touch him.

Her hand reached out almost against her will, and she touched him, there…at his core. It was real, it was life affirming.

"Megan."

Nine

Passion ripped through his taut form, scorching him with fire, filling him with a yearning need that he'd never known.

Shafir couldn't have stopped himself kissing Megan if a hurricane had arrived.

He licked at her soft, moist lips. Heard her groan and felt her body arch against him. And that set off another explosion of heat.

He went rigid.

"I suppose you're going to tell me I should not be doing this. If you are, stop me now."

"Do it again," she said hoarsely.

His hands stroked up her arms and over her naked shoulders in long, slow sweeps that roused shivers of endless pleasure. His fingers played a game of erotic tag against her spine.

Her hand clenched around his hard length, making him

convulse with pleasure, the black swimsuit offering little protection.

Water lapped against his sleek, naked skin. His legs, corded with muscle, brushed against hers. The contrast of male and female, hard and soft, the sensual whisper of the water all conspired to make him harden against her fingers.

She brought him out of the swimsuit. "I want you," she murmured as he gasped against her mouth. "Now."

"It will be over in a minute if you carry on."

"I don't care."

Her fingers drove him insane. He threw back his head and squeezed his eyes shut and, holding his breath, waited for the starbursts.

It came too suddenly, a wild moment of sharp, escalating pleasure that left him aching for more.

Before she could move away, he clasped his hands around her hips and hoisted her onto the edge of the poolside.

"Put your hands behind you and brace yourself."

"Shafir! What are you doing?"

"Your turn now."

Her breath caught, the sound loud in the stillness of the Garden of Pools. "I've already had my turn."

"The pleasure was all mine…none belonged to you."

Her dark eyes were wild with emotion. "But the satisfaction was mine. I needed to know that you are functioning. That you are safe."

"Oh, Megan."

Driven to desperation by the words that tugged at his heart, he rose up out of the water and his mouth closed over the tight nipples covered by the clinging, wet Lycra bikini.

It was her turn to gasp, and the hoarse sound filled him with soaring pleasure. One hand slid under the bottom of edge of the suit, sliding over the base of the breast his mouth sucked.

Cupping the heavy warmth of her breast, he massaged the voluptuous flesh while his tongue played across the rigid tip, separated from her skin only by a barrier of thin cloth.

Megan flung her head back, sounds of ecstasy escaping her.

It was time.

Sliding back into the pool, freeing his hand, Shafir dropped lower. The curve of her mons under the swimsuit drew his eye. She was exquisite. Pressing openmouthed kisses over the mound that her bikini bottoms concealed, he stroked the firm flesh of her belly until she moaned with delight.

Lifting his head, he hooked his thumbs over the edges of her bikini bottoms and pulled them off.

She was so sweet. He tasted her, kissed her, until she spasmed beneath his mouth, her thighs trembling around him.

When he raised his head, her gaze met his, dark and slumberous in the twilight. "And don't you dare tell me tomorrow that I imagined this," she said, "that it's nothing more than a fantasy fueled by my feminine mind."

That night, lying alone in the darkness of bedchamber, Shafir thought about the softness of her skin, the silky hair, the scent of her and tried to make sense of what the hell had happened out there in the Garden of Pools.

Don't you dare tell me tomorrow that I imagined this.

Oh, hell.

He hadn't lost control and spilled himself like that since he'd taken his first woman. What power did Megan Saxon hold over him?

A fantasy fueled by my feminine mind.

Her biting words had shaken him. As, no doubt, she'd meant them to. He saw with utter clarity that Megan had told him the truth about Jacques—the man had been two-timing Zara and Megan. He'd arrogantly chosen to disregard it—had attributed it to frivolity—and now he had to deal with the fallout.

He couldn't bear to think of her performing such intimacies with Jacques...or any man. This woman had been made for him.

His brain must be heat crazed. He was going mad!

It was almost possible to believe she was a *houri* who promised him all the pleasures of paradise. The sound choked out of him didn't resemble humor.

Surrounded by darkness, he remembered his grandmother telling him of how Sheherazade had spun tales that had saved her from certain death and mesmerized the hapless sultan each night. Megan reduced him to being her captive with ease.

Entertain me.

But he hadn't meant for her to turn him to putty in her hands. Hell, he couldn't think straight.

For the first time in his life Shafir found himself in a situation where sensual pleasure ruled. In the past, he'd been driven by clear, cold intellect. Yet now all he could think of was Megan. Making love to Megan. Talking to Megan. Filling his life with Megan.

In the past few hours he'd even started to have traitorous thoughts about asking her to stay with him in Dhahara, to be his lover. If he did what his senses craved, his family would think she'd made him as crazy as they believed her to be.

What a mess!

At last, after much tossing and turning, a little after midnight, he came to a decision.

Tomorrow he would return to the city. He would confront Garnier—and then he would face the difficult task of telling Zara the unpalatable truth.

And then he would need to find the strength to apologize to Megan for misjudging her.

She would have every right to call him a bastard.

The limousine cut a straight track through the desert as though the hounds of hell were on their tail.

"Why the hurry?" asked Megan, slanting a glance to the man beside her.

Shafir had been silent, brooding, since they'd parted last night.

Last night...

Megan didn't want to think about last night. The shivery pleasure. The heat that had scorched her. The cool silkiness of the water and the heat of his mouth.

Oh, dear God, how would she ever forget it?

"I am needed in the capital. For a meeting," he said abruptly.

She yanked herself back to the present. "Today?"

"Tomorrow."

She wouldn't be surprised if the meeting had been hurriedly set up this morning—if it existed at all. She didn't believe for a moment that a meeting was the reason for their return to Katar.

She considered, and abandoned, the idea that the events in the pool last night might be responsible for this rush from Qasr Al-Ward. Shafir was not a man governed by passion. He was much too hard and fierce. No, this must have to do with his family, with his cousin's wedding.

She was shaken by how little she'd wanted to leave the palace, the surrounding desert, and venture back into the city. Her memories of Dhahara would be colored by the world Shafir had shown her. She would treasure those.

"If you only need to attend a meeting tomorrow, then surely we can slow down to ensure Your Highness makes it back in one piece?"

He glowered at her sarcasm.

The limousine swerved. Megan clutched the edge of her seat. "There. See, that's what I mean."

Shafir bent forward and yanked open the window to the driver's compartment and spoke in rapid-fire Arabic. Megan caught *"shway shway."* Slowly. She relaxed a little.

"It was a camel."

"A camel?"

"A wild camel in the road."

"Oh, no. Did we hit it?" She hadn't felt any impact.

"No, no. There are lots of wild camels. The desert is full of them."

"I've fallen in love with your camels. I think it's their eyes…and those beautiful eyelashes."

"I thought you said it was their soft noses that appealed to you."

"Oh, it's everything about them."

Shafir couldn't believe that he was being sucked into a discussion about the appeal of camels, of all creatures.

At last he said, "There is a camel stud farm not far from here where they breed racing camels."

"Oh, please, can we go look?"

Shafir's lips compressed.

"Don't worry," Megan said, and sank back against the plush seat, closing her eyes to shut him out. "I know, you have a meeting."

An hour later the limousine slowed and Shafir watched as Megan's eyelashes fluttered up.

She stretched her arms up and the curve of her breasts rose against the shirt she wore.

He stifled a moan.

"You're awake."

Catching his gaze on her, she paused in midstretch. Her arms fell to her sides and Shafir sighed with regret.

"How far are we from Katar? Why are we slowing?"

"We're at the camel stud farm."

"But I thought—" Midsentence she stopped. "Thank you, Shafir."

Her face lit up, and for a moment he thought she was going to hurl herself across the seat at him. He tensed in anticipation. But at the last moment she cast him an uncertain smile. "I can't wait."

"Be careful," he warned. "Camels are moody animals, they can be fierce and troublesome."

"I know all about fierce and troublesome animals." And she shot him a look that was full of wicked humor.

Shafir couldn't decide whether he should shout with laughter or scold her severely. Or simply kiss her.

There were more camels at the stud farm than Shafir had ever seen in one place before, and Megan seemed to want to examine each one.

The wealthy, fleshy Arab who owned the farm was examining Megan with lazy approval. "You like what you see," he tossed out.

"I am not certain," Shafir bit out.

The breeder caught Shafir's dangerous glare and froze. Making a hasty excuse, he took himself off in a hurry.

"Jerk," murmured Shafir.

"Who? The breeder?" Megan turned to him. "I thought he was very helpful."

"Too damned helpful," he muttered.

But her gaze was on the camels. "Oh, Shafir, look at the young camel there. The pale one."

"He is too pale for the desert. He will suffer in the sun."

"Oh, the poor thing." Megan looked worried.

He rapped out an instruction to a man by the fence. Minutes later the camel stood before Megan, a groom at its head.

"Oh, look at the tufts of hair on its head, and its nose feels like velvet. Shafir, it's gorgeous."

"He."

"He?" A furrow appeared between her eyes.

"He, not *it*."

"Oh…am I insulting your manhood, boy?" she murmured to the camel.

The camel buried his head against her shirt and Shafir decided that the camel was a male after his own heart.

Afterward while Megan returned to the limousine, despite his raised hackles, Shafir had a few surreptitious words with the breeder to secure a price for the camel and arrange to have it delivered. Not that he needed another camel.

Not that Megan would ever know he'd bought it…or even see the animal she had fallen in love with.

It was highly unlikely that she would be visiting Qasr Al-Ward again. But he would have a concrete symbol to remind him of her. And he knew that this camel would be the most spoiled animal that had ever wandered the Dhaharan desert.

Two days later Shafir threw his pen down and stared out the window of the spacious library that doubled as a study in his city home and sighed.

He was running out of time. Jacques Garnier appeared

to have vanished off the face of the earth, and Shafir was having a devil of a time tracking him down. Instead of confronting Garnier, all he seemed to be doing was thinking of Megan every waking moment. Wondering what she was doing when he was out, if she was bored, if she was missing the gardens of Qasr Al-Ward. And when he would manage to screw up the guts to apologize to her...

She'd assured him that she wasn't bored. He knew she'd discovered his library and had spent hours hidden away, reading memoirs and books about Dhahara, as well as some of the Jack Reacher novels he possessed.

A rap on the door interrupted his thoughts and he sat up in anticipation.

Megan.

To his disappointment, Zara swept in, followed by his aunt Lily. Quashing the feeling of anticlimax, he rose to his feet with a welcoming smile.

"I'm sorry, Your Highness." His city aide's worried face appeared around the doorjamb. "They didn't wait to be announced."

Shafir waved the aide away. But his smile faded as he took in his cousin's pale face.

Shock? Had Zara encountered Megan in the house? Had she known who Megan was? Dear Allah, he hoped not.

"What brings you here, Zara?" he asked, rapidly deciding that he couldn't tell her the truth before he'd confronted Garnier. "Are you not caught up in the throes of last-minute arrangements for the wedding?"

"There is going to be no wedding," Zara declared dramatically.

Aunt Lily closed her eyes in resignation. Clearly she'd heard this already.

Shafir froze. "What do you mean?"

"Jacques is going to jilt me."

His first thought was of Megan. Was it possible that she'd made contact with Jacques Garnier in the two days since they'd arrived in the city? Had she threatened Garnier if he didn't call the wedding off? His first reaction was denial. Megan had been quite definite that she never wanted to see Garnier again.

But it was possible that she might have relished threatening this man. A heaviness settled in his stomach at the very thought. He would discuss it with her later.

What if she had seen Jacques?

What if Jacques tried to convince her she meant something to him? He hoped she would not be swayed.

He pushed it out his mind. For now he had to get to the bottom of the immediate crisis.

"Garnier has told you he's jilting you?"

"Not in so many words."

Tapping his fingers against his thigh, he studied Zara through contemplative eyes. "So what makes you so certain he intends to call it off?"

"He has another woman."

His fingers stilled. "You have proof of this?"

"I have heard that he has a woman." She gave a sob. "I asked him if it was true. He says he loves only me."

So Zara knew where the Frenchman was. "But you don't believe him?"

"I no longer know what to believe."

Focussing all his attention on his cousin, he asked, "What do you mean?"

"There was that other woman who was stalking him…now there is this hussy who I hear he is having an affair with. I don't like it."

Shafir didn't like it, either. But at least it meant Megan

hadn't been to see Garnier. Zara was talking of someone else. The relief that swept over Shafir was overwhelming.

Not that he'd ever believed Megan would take up with Garnier again…but she was quite capable of threatening him.

"Zara," her mother interjected, "Jacques is a wealthy man, and he is going to be pursued by women. There will always be rumors. You will have to get used to it. You must trust him—you are to be married."

"I don't know if I do anymore. What if these women are the same person? What if he was never being stalked at all and Jacques is making a fool of me? Lying to me for the sake of his whore?"

"Zara!" Shafir thundered. "I do not want to hear such talk." A fierce protective emotion swamped him. He would allow no one—not even his dearest cousin—to talk about Megan in such a manner.

"But who else will listen to me?"

Pity for Zara filled him. "Cousin, do you love this man?"

"Yes!"

"You want to spend your life with him, grow old with him?"

She looked at him as though he'd grown horns. "Why else would I marry him?"

"There are lots of reasons people get married, and they are not always the right ones."

"I love Jacques."

"Then he is a lucky man. And before you jump to conclusions about another woman, consider whether he would do such a thing if he loves you." But Shafir knew there was no conviction in his words. He knew that the gossip was probably correct. He would be making discreet inquiries about exactly whom Jacques had been meeting.

If Zara still wanted to marry the man knowing what he'd

done, then by Allah he'd make Garnier understand there would be no more affairs or flirtations. Ever. Not unless he wanted to end his chances of begetting sons.

Shafir had just seen Zara and his aunt Lily off when the king arrived with his phalanx of security guards. Leaving the guards patrolling the perimeter of the property, the king entered the house and demanded to know why Shafir was back in the city.

"Business, Father."

"And the woman? Where is she?" His father looked around the entrance hall and up and down the staircase as if expecting Megan to emerge at any second.

It struck Shafir that he hadn't seen Megan for a while.

"Do not concern yourself with the woman, Father." A note of irony crept into his voice as he echoed his father's "the woman."

His father frowned, his astute eyes examining Shafir with fierce attention.

It was a standing joke that the king knew what would happen in Dhahara before perpetrators had even decided to commit a crime. Now Shafir wondered if the king knew something he didn't. Had Megan indeed been in contact with Garnier, and had the king's force of aides and guards discovered it?

"You have changed."

"No, Father, I am still your son."

The king harrumped. "I hear from my guards that this woman is living with you in your house here in the city."

That was it.

Shafir bowed his head in assent, relieved that his apprehensions that Megan had been seen meeting with Jacques had been unfounded.

"Come, Father, let us sit in comfort."

"It is dangerous for her to be here in the city. Zara could find out—"

"Zara will discover nothing!"

"It will be easier for this woman to contact Zara, to make trouble."

Shafir's patience snapped. "Do not refer to her as 'this woman.' She has a name—Megan." He held his father's gaze. "She will not make trouble. She is not the type."

"She is a lunatic."

"She is far from crazy."

"You disagree with me to defend this woman?"

"She wasn't stalking Jacques—he made that up."

"Why would he lie?"

Shafir gave his father a very male look. "Why do you think?"

"You mean—"

Shafir nodded and ushered his father into the library.

"Oh." The king appeared at a loss for words. He walked across the Persian rug and settled himself on a chair with an upright back. "But such a woman shouldn't be living in your house."

He'd found something to say soon enough, Shafir thought with grim humor as he leaned against the desk and crossed one ankle over the other. He refrained from pointing out that the reason Megan was staying in his house at all was because the king had ordered him to keep her from making mischief in any way he chose. Which he had done.

"People will think—"

"I don't care what people think."

"You think it doesn't matter what people think, my son?" King Selim gave a sigh.

"They call me the untamed one. I have more freedom than Khalid."

"You know they call you that? You think it is a good thing?" His father shook his head. "I am not sure. I wish your mother were alive. I could do with her counsel now."

For the first time Shafir realized that his father was getting older. There were lines across his forehead that he was certain hadn't been there only months ago.

"If your mother were here she would've known what to do about this woman—"

"Megan!"

"About this Megan." His father pinched the bridge of his nose. "Khalid and you would both have been married by now. She would have arranged it."

With difficulty Shafir stopped himself from rolling his eyes. Instead he folded his arms, and said defensively, "I can find my own wife."

"But you are tardy in doing so, my son. And having this woman staying in your home is not going to help find you a wife." Another heavy sigh accompanied this observation. "And it might come to Zara's attention—she would be upset. You know how fond she is of you."

"There's no reason for her to link Megan to Jacques Garnier, unless someone tells her. And I have done everything possible to keep her out of the way so that nothing can endanger Zara's marriage to Garnier." He didn't add that he'd had an awful moment when he thought that Zara had bumped into Megan earlier. Nor did he add that he would be taking care of Jacques. No point in alarming his father further.

"But—"

"Megan is a nice woman, Father."

"I don't think—"

"You should meet her." He steamrolled over his father's objections. "Perhaps we can all dine together one night?"

The king looked horrified. "I don't want to meet this woman who causes such misery."

"Megan. Her name is Megan. Say it."

"Megan," said the king with utter reluctance.

"Our family has done her a grave wrong. The very least we can do is acknowledge her."

"A grave wrong?" The king grew more horrified. "Oh, no. You did what Rafiq suggested! You seduced this woman to keep her mind off Jacques."

Shafir raised his hand. "Enough."

"Ay, me." The king threw his hands into the air. "I can listen no more. I told you to keep this woman out of the way until the wedding was over. You have disobeyed me."

In all his life he had never deliberately disobeyed the king. But he had brought Megan back to the city against his father's dictates.

Because he had wanted to deal with Garnier.

"Father, I did not seduce her—"

King Selim was on his feet. "I can see from your face that there is something between you. You cannot lie to me, my son. She is your mistress."

He hesitated too long before denying it. "No, I have not asked her to be my mistress."

And suddenly he was fiercely glad that he had not done so.

Megan deserved better.

His father stalked closer and, putting his face close to Shafir's, he said, "You have chosen to bring her to the city, to live unchaperoned with her in your home, to bring shame on your family."

"Father—"

"But you will obey me in this, my son. You will keep her away from the wedding, even if that means you do not attend yourself."

Before he could draw a breath and tell his father that there might not be a wedding—unless Zara demanded it— the king had turned on his heel and stormed out of the library. Anger rising, Shafir strode after him.

"Father, her name has been dragged through the mud by a—"

The front door slammed. The entrance hall was empty. The king had gone.

Ten

Framed in the doorway of the library, Shafir halted mid-step as Megan spoke into the prickling silence: "So you planned to seduce me to keep me away from Jacques?"

Hampered by her long skirt, she clambered down from the little suspended loft where she'd been curled up reading when Zara and Lily had entered the room. Once they'd started speaking, she'd been trapped.

Facing a fiercely frowning Shafir, she refused to be intimated by the grandeur he radiated in his sparkling white thobe, his swathe of overlong hair brushing past his collar. "Am I to understand that you planned everything that happened beside the pool at the Palace of Roses?" The extent of the hurt and betrayal that rolled inside her took Megan by surprise.

"Have you been here all the time?"

She could see him rapidly trying to recall all that had been said, everything damaging she might have heard.

"Oh, yes. I heard about your brother's idea for you to seduce me so that I would forget all about Jacques and wouldn't threaten Zara's wedding."

Glowering at her, clearly hating being caught in the wrong, he walked slowly into the room. "You should've made your presence known."

"And spoil the fun? I didn't get the chance. How could I emerge when Zara had just announced that Jacques was jilting her? How do you think she would've felt to know that a stranger had witnessed her humiliation? But it's just as well I stayed, because I learned so much." The searing hurt was awful. So much worse than when she'd discovered the truth about how Jacques had been jerking her around. What had happened in the Garden of Pools had been special.

Or so she'd thought.

"I hope you found it entertaining," she spat out.

Four long strides brought him to a halt in front of her. He stretched out a conciliatory hand. "Megan—"

She slapped his hand away and retreated to stand beside the couch. "Don't 'Megan' me."

Drawing a deep breath, she raked her fingers through her long hair and fought for composure. She would not let him see her fall apart. She could cry later.

When she was alone.

"You planned with your brother how you were going to seduce me."

"I di—"

"How dare you do such a thing?"

She let the rage that had been festering for weeks loose. His abduction of her. Jacques's betrayal of her. It all erupted.

"You didn't know me, had never seen me." Something flared in his eyes. "You knew what I looked like," she said slowly.

"I saw photos."

"Photos? Where did you get photos of me?"

Shafir shrugged. "My father has security resources—"

"You *spied* on me?"

"Not me."

"Your family spied on me. Oh, God, I'm going to be sick."

"Sit down, before you fall down. You look like you're going to faint," he said with brutal frankness.

Megan sank onto the sofa. She did feel ill; her stomach was churning. It would serve him right if she vomited all over the Persian rug that she suspected was worth a fortune. "You are despicable. You're all despicable."

"I never planned to seduce you." Shafir leaned back against the desk and folded his arms across his chest. "In fact, when Rafiq suggested it, I told him that I would never sink that low."

"Well, you appear to have forgotten your good intentions!" She was too fired up to acknowledge that she'd played a big part in what had happened at the pool.

"Megan, what you and I did—"

She bent her head and stared at the flat gold leather sandals she wore. "I don't want to talk about it."

"We have to."

She shook her head, "No, I want to talk about what your father believes. He said—"

"A lot of things. All of them based on incorrect assumptions. And I defended you."

That brought her gaze back to his face. She searched his features, looking for the truth. "Not that I heard."

"You must have heard me say that you were a nice woman. We weren't in the library for the rest."

"How convenient."

Shafir had given her exquisite pleasure, without feeling a shred of any softer emotion for her. She felt used. Even though she knew she was probably overreacting, given that she'd started the chain of events that had culminated in this.

But she'd been so scared for him that day.

Terrified by what might have happened out there in the desert. The bandits might have killed him.

It mattered. Because somehow she'd grown to care for him.

And that made her feel even sicker. Heartsick.

Oh, Lord, please not heartsick.

She clamped her arms across her stomach. How could she have been such a fool? For a second time? *Fool me once, shame on you, fool me twice, shame on me.* But this time she hadn't been in love with the idea of being in love; this time the emotion that twisted her heart was so much more powerful.

And this time she'd picked a man who could marry up to four wives if he chose. A man who lived in a country a world away from her own, where most of the inhabitants couldn't speak English.

A man who described her only as *nice*.

She was asking for heartbreak.

"And your cousin—" she forced herself to look at him without revealing the shuddering shock of realization "—she shares some of these misapprehensions about me?"

Shafir's sigh said it all.

"So she does. Tell me what I'm supposed to have done to merit such antagonism. I have a right to know."

So he told her how his father had discovered her impending arrival and had feared that she planned to stop the wedding between Jacques and Zara.

Megan perched on the edge of the sofa. "He just assumed I would do that?"

"Garnier confirmed it."

"Jacques did?"

How many shocks was she going to have to bear?

"You mean, he was asked about me right in the beginning, before you abducted me?"

Shafir nodded, and she glimpsed distaste in his eyes. Despite his casual posture against the desk, his folded arms, she could detect his tension. "Zara found missed calls from you on his phone. She confronted him. He told her you were a business colleague who'd turned into a crazy stalker."

"Me? Stalking him?" She thought about his smooth approach the first time they'd met, his offer to buy her a drink, his intent gaze as he'd spun her a line about how she had to be his soul mate.

She'd swallowed it hook, line and sinker.

The rat!

A clever rat, because in ten minutes flat he'd discerned what she'd been seeking. A soul mate. She hadn't even known it herself...

If Jacques hadn't lied, Shafir would never have kidnapped her. She might never have met him.

Megan shot Shafir a sideways look. Despite his ruthlessness, she knew he would *never* prey on a woman's most secret needs like that.

"You know, if I were Zara, I'd want to know that Jacques lied about those calls without blinking. I'd want to know that he is a two-timing rat."

"Zara has already heard rumors of a woman, you heard that. Yet she says she loves Jacques. If he hurts her after their marriage he will pay—Rafiq and I will make sure he understands that."

"Would you care if your woman had another man?"

Dark heat flared in his eyes. "Of course I'd care. I'd want her to be mine, only mine."

"Would you grant her the same courtesy?" Megan held her breath.

"I've told you before that when I find a woman special enough, I would forsake all others."

"Forever?"

He tilted his head in that familiar half-nod and stared at her from narrowed, inscrutable eyes. "Forever."

The breath Megan had been holding escaped in a rush.

"And, believe me, it will be forever. For both of us." His expression was fierce, his mouth passionate. "My woman will not need to seek love elsewhere."

Megan believed him.

Lucky woman.

But that woman could never be her.

He thought she was nice. Nothing more. She fixed her gaze on her sandals again. He was nothing like Jacques. He would be more true than her father had been.

Even though Shafir had kidnapped her, taken her to his palace, it had been done for his family. Because it was what his father wanted. Because he loved his cousin and didn't want to see her hurt.

Megan could see it all so clearly now.

But she needed to know more. Lifting her head, she asked, "When I said I wanted to go home, you refused to let me. At first you believed I might generate adverse publicity and jeopardise Zara's wedding. Then you came up with another ploy."

"It wasn't a ploy."

"Wasn't it?" She waited a beat, then asked softly, "So why did you keep me here?"

"I told you, I wanted to change your mind about Dhahara. I couldn't let you leave with the impression you'd gained of the country and people." But he glanced away and flicked nonexistent dust from the front of his thobe. "Okay, maybe I wasn't…" His voice trailed away.

"Honest? You're not telling me everything. I think you

wanted an excuse to keep me close. I think you wanted to keep me under observation."

She waited for a long moment.

"Nothing more to say? Well then, I suppose that's it then."

She got to her feet.

"It's all been about Zara's precious wedding, making sure that nothing happens to undo that. I hope she appreciates the lengths you've gone to for her. Kidnapping—"

"Megan—"

"—Seducing the enemy—"

"Megan!"

He'd straightened and was no longer leaning idly against the desk.

"It's true." She shook her head and her long hair, unconstrained by a *hijab,* whipped against her face. "I'm so sick of all the doublespeak, all the lies."

She walked to where he stood.

"Shafir, I've had enough. I want to go home. And this time nothing is going to stop me."

She wanted to leave.

As Megan's words sank in, something tore deep inside Shafir's chest. He was not losing her. Megan was not walking out on him; he would not allow it.

A dark emotion swarmed over him. "So you think I'm the enemy? You think I set out to deliberately seduce you?"

She shrugged. "Seduce…make love…what's the difference?"

Her attitude sparked the first real flare of anger. "There's a world of difference between what happened in the Garden of Pools and a calculated seduction."

"You think?" She swung away and headed for the door. But he leaped across the room and got there first.

Slamming the heavy door shut, he locked it and said, "I'll show you the difference."

She glared up at him. "Get out of my way."

He didn't answer. Instead, he cupped his hand beneath her jaw and stroked the soft, sensitive skin behind her ears. Using every ounce of sensual skill he possessed he worked on making her aware of him in a deeply primal way. He knew he'd won when she quivered under his fingertips.

"See? Your body betrays you," he said roughly. "I knew you would respond if I touched you like this…and this."

"Shafir!" She leaned weakly against the door, horrified by the breathiness in her own voice, hating herself for responding so readily to his high-handedness.

His hands slid up under the T-shirt she wore and stripped it over her head in one quick move. She wore no bra. Excitement surged through her. He cupped her breast and, before she could think of objecting, his head dropped. He teased the hard pebble of her nipple with light flicks of his tongue.

Waves of delight pulsed through her. The heavy wood of the door was cool and hard against her naked back. Her knees had gone weak and her body had acquired a disturbing will of its own.

When he lifted his head, Megan saw that his hair was rumpled and his fierce bronze eyes burned.

His fingers pushed down the elastic waistband of her swirling skirt. A twist of the panties she wore and the lace snapped.

Before she could murmur more than a half-hearted objection he stroked her intimately, his fingers finding the secret furrow and sliding back and forth to create a delicious friction. Closing her eyes, she moaned as those knowing fingers slid into her, stroking her, heating her, until her hips arched away from the door.

She was breathing heavily.

He moved away from her and her eyes cracked open in time to see him shuck off the thobe, the white T-shirt beneath and the long, soft, white cotton pants he wore. The last item to land on the heap were his boxers.

He stood before her, naked, virile and one hundred percent male.

Shafir stepped forward, his thigh pushing between hers. Meeting with the obstruction of her silky skirt, he eased the garment further down over her legs. Bare legs tangled.

Hers soft and feminine, his hard and muscled.

Circling her hips with his hands, he lifted her, holding her in place against the door. Megan moved, rocked against him, and his erection settled against the junction of her thighs.

Shafir groaned out loud.

Holding her tightly, he slid forward into her heat. Deep. Dark. And incredibly dangerous…

He hadn't used protection.

Hell. The instant he thought it, he tried to pull out. She wound her legs around his hips. His brain melted as she started to move. The hot friction. The pure, passionate pleasure. The explosive heat. It all swirled around him like the bright, bold colors of a kaleidoscope.

Bending his head, he covered her mouth with his and tasted her.

The peaks of pleasure built rapidly. He cried out as she shuddered around him, and he came into her in a series of short, sharp bursts.

Afterward, Shafir turned away from her, filled with soul-destroying guilt.

He couldn't bring himself to meet her eyes, so hot with passion. He'd used the simmering attraction between them to seduce her. Seduce her in icy anger to underscore his point.

He'd set out to show her what it felt like to be seduced.

He had taken her uncaring of their surroundings, uncaring of her comfort, and he had striven only for the quick pleasure of immediate gratification. He had played her body expertly, tempting her with sensation, and Megan had never stood a chance of resisting him.

How could he have neglected to use protection?

He'd never taken such a risk before.

Shame swept him.

Picking her T-shirt up off the floor, he handed it to her. Her lashes veiled her eyes as she scooped up her skirt and tugged it on. He glanced away from the scraps of devastated lace that had been her briefs.

"I told my father that you had been wronged by our family," he said lamely.

"I heard something to that effect."

"I have wronged you, too. Both in the past by thinking you'd misinterpreted Jacques's manners for something more, and just now."

"Shafir—"

With difficulty he met her eyes. There was none of the fury he expected. She looked bewildered—and vulnerable.

His heart contracted. "Megan, I am sorry. I don't expect you to forgive me for what just happened—"

"I could have said no," she pointed out.

The first stirring of hope awakened. Passion so perfect could not end like this. Perhaps he hadn't lost her yet. Then he remembered that she wanted to go home. He had lost her.

But first, his family owed her an apology.

"Before you leave, I am going to arrange for you to meet my family." Shafir made the announcement that following morning after breakfast as they sipped the Arabian coffee that Hanif had prepared.

It was the remorse Shafir exhibited that triggered the realization of how much she loved him. But Megan gave a laugh that was half groan. "Oh, Shafir. It's far from that easy."

He set down his cup. "What's hard about it?"

"Your father thinks that associating with me will ruin you. I'm not the kind of woman he wants you to marry."

Then she flushed, because marriage had never even been mentioned.

Keep your mouth shut, she told herself. Megan had no illusions about the chances of survival of a relationship between herself and Shafir.

He was a desert prince.

She wasn't exactly a pauper—her family was extremely wealthy in their own right—but his father was a king with the wealth of Croesus and they lived in palaces and jetted around in private jets.

The woman whom Shafir married would need to have been groomed for the position from birth.

But instead of laughing at her, he said, "Well, he's certainly never managed to produce the kind of woman that I do want to marry."

She'd overheard something along those lines yesterday. "In the library your father wished your mother was here." She paused, searching for the right words. Aniya had said something weeks ago in passing that had suggested Shafir and his brothers had no mother.

"She's dead," he said abruptly.

"I'm sorry." He'd listened to her talk about the problems between her parents, her grief at the death of her brother. But she'd never asked him about his mother. Suddenly Megan felt very small. "I'm so sorry."

"It was a long time ago."

She suspected he needed time, that this was not an easy subject for him. She took a quick sip of the strong, dark Arabian coffee and returned to the subject that was clear-cut. "I need to move out of your home. I heard your father saying you wouldn't be welcome at your cousin's wedding. If I go, that will change."

He held her gaze. "In case you've forgotten, the reason you're with me in the first place is because I kidnapped you because of that damned wedding. My father can't change the tune now. And the wedding might not even happen. If Zara has any sense, she will agree to call it off after I've dealt with Jacques."

"Still, if the wedding goes forward, I'm the last woman in the world your family will want to meet."

"They will love you once they get to know you." An aura of absolute certainty surrounded him. Once she'd called it arrogance. "You will see."

She wished she could share his confidence. Instead she sighed and pushed the empty cup away. "There's no point to all this, Shafir. I am leaving. You're making waves with your family for no reason."

She wasn't ready to face the thought of leaving.

But she had to.

She'd come starry-eyed to Dhahara on a quest to find excitement, adventure and romance. Yet instead of love, Jacques had betrayed her. She'd been so gullible, and had vowed never again. Her trust in her own judgment had been shattered.

And now that it was time to leave, she'd fallen in love—real love—with the sheik she'd so scornfully dismissed as a savage.

The irony.

"You need to meet my family." His dark eyebrows formed a formidable frown. "I'd say that Jacques's muddying your name and my family all believing it is reason enough."

So this had to do with his concept of honor.

It made her love him even more.

But she couldn't help wishing he'd been doing all this because he loved her in return, rather than because he felt obliged to right a wrong.

But however much she valued the gesture, she couldn't let him alienate himself from his family only for the sake of a nice woman's tarnished reputation.

"And the sooner my family realizes that I will not miss Zara's wedding—and you will be attending with me—the better."

The flat gaze warned her that he was deadly serious. He would put her ahead of his family's and Zara's wishes.

Oh, but she was tempted....

She drew a shuddering breath. "I will refuse."

There was no other choice.

His eyes narrowed to metallic chinks. "Because of Jacques?"

Annoyance flared. "How many times do I need to tell you I don't care about Jacques anymore? I won't go because of *you*. Your father is right. Our association will do you no good."

Her stomach rolled over as their eyes remained locked.

It would be so easy to say yes, so easy to admit her love and never leave....

But she owed him more.

Later that day Megan had been told by an excited Naema, who had arrived in Katar a few days after she had, that the sheik was taking her out to dinner.

Megan wondered if taking her out on the town was an attempt to flaunt her presence in the city. Despite his father's orders, it certainly looked like Shafir had no intention of keeping her hidden. She'd considered refusing—for his own good. But in the end, she'd been too weak to resist what would have to be the first and final night out with him.

She'd soaked in the tub and Naema had rubbed scented oils into her skin afterward. Megan was feeling gloriously relaxed by the time Naema laid out her clothes.

"Don't you think that is too ornate?" She eyed the yellow caftan with gold thread on the bed. It had arrived in a box tied with gold ribbons.

"No. It's perfect, and it comes with this." Naema held up a fine piece of silk. "For your head," she explained.

By the time Megan was dressed, she was sure it was all too much. But Naema wouldn't hear a word of it. "This is what His Highness wanted you to wear tonight."

"Prince Shafir chose my clothes?"

The young woman looked apprehensive. "Yes."

But once she got downstairs, she was glad she'd let Naema sway her. Shafir looked magnificent in a richly embroidered thobe that made him appear…princely… and emphasized the gulf that yawned between them.

Shafir wasn't terribly forthcoming about where they were going when he led her out to the waiting limousine. The first inkling she had that this was more than a dinner date was when the car drew up outside an elaborate white marble building that glowed like a pearl in the evening light.

Megan did a double take. "I've seen photos of this—it's the official state palace of King Selim."

"Yes, it is."

It was the lack of inflection in his voice that caused reality to penetrate. She turned to him. "Tell me we're not about to visit your father."

"Don't worry, we won't be alone. My brothers will be there, too. We're going to dinner."

"Oh, no." She raised a hand to cover her mouth. "Shafir, you should've warned me."

"And have you refuse to come? It's easier this way."

"Easier?" Her voice rose. "Easier for whom?"

"For you. Otherwise you would have fretted."

"Are you surprised? It's not every day that I get to meet a king. You could've given me time to prepare."

"What's to prepare? He's just a man."

"A very powerful man," she corrected. And he was Shafir's father. A father who already disapproved of her.

"Relax," Shafir urged.

She resisted the impulse to snort. And then there was no more time for talk because the vehicle had pulled up beside a grand set of stairs and the chauffeur had opened the door.

Megan focused on slow, deep breaths as she passed through the arched doorway. The entrance lobby was lit with hundreds of candles, and the corridor they took seemed to go on for miles before they reached a salon.

Noise and a blur of color bombarded her, before it separated itself into a group of people. An older man, two tall men, one accompanied by a tiny, beautiful, delicate creature with cat-green eyes and a pouting mouth.

Megan hesitated. Then she squared her shoulders and strode forward. Dammit, she'd done nothing wrong.

At the last moment she realized that she'd forgotten to ask Shafir if she was supposed to curtsy, or what, when introduced to the king. Her stomach balled with nerves.

Be yourself, she decided.

So she smiled as the king stepped forward.

He inspected her with sharp eyes that she guessed missed very little.

"My father, His Royal Highness, King Selim al Dhahara." Megan found she was shaking, and her hand trembled as the king lifted it and bowed over it in an old-fashioned courtly gesture.

She was relieved when Shafir finally led her over and introduced her to his brothers and Rafiq's girlfriend.

The ribbing and jokes surprised her. The family was tight-knit.

Everywhere Megan went she was aware of the King's gaze following her. She knew he wished to protect his son. Yet the tension between the king and Shafir was palpable.

And despite everyone's smiles and well-mannered small talk, misery overwhelmed Megan.

She was the cause of this rift between father and son.

And everyone here knew it.

Eleven

Dinner passed in a haze of careful politeness. The food was beautifully prepared, but it could've been sawdust for all Megan knew. She barely tasted it.

Once coffee had been served and the robed manservant had retreated, Megan comforted herself with the promise that the evening would soon be over. But even as her anxiety finally began to settle, a commotion behind her caused her to look to the doorway.

Two women entered the long dining hall. The younger was striking. Of medium height, she was slender and moved with easy grace. A gauzy chiffon scarf was draped around her neck, and the lights of the chandeliers picked out gold highlights in her tawny hair. The second woman was older. But the high cheekbones and delicate bone structure marked her as the younger woman's mother.

Megan's heart sank.

Beside her she felt Shafir stiffen.

This must be Zara, and the older woman would be her mother, Lily.

There was an awkward silence as the women came toward them, and Megan pretended not to see the glances that were flashed her way.

"I have something to tell you all." Zara's announcement broke the taut stillness.

"We have a visitor with us tonight," said Shafir interrupting.

"Oh." She paused, and her curious brown eyes fell on Megan. Then she smiled. "I am Zara."

Megan smiled back. Zara was lovely, with a delicate gazelle-like femininity that made it easy to see why Shafir was so protective of her.

"It's nice to meet you, Zara. I'm Megan."

"Megan?" Zara's eyes grew curious. Then she stepped forward.

The silence that followed pressed against Megan's eardrums. Zara *must* know, she thought.

"I'm sorry for interrupting your dinner."

The whole room seemed to let out a collective sigh of relief.

Megan wanted to laugh at the absurdity of Zara's apology. She was hardly an honored guest. "We've already finished. And I think it's probably time for me to leave." She glanced a little desperately at Shafir.

But he didn't move.

"Oh, I don't want to break up the party."

Did Zara know who she was? Apparently not. But this uncomfortable situation could hardly be described as a party. And Megan was relieved when Shafir said, "You haven't crashed a party."

"Good." Zara moved over to where the King sat at the

head of the table. "Because I didn't want you to have another reason to be angry with me, Uncle Selim."

"What is it, child?" Concern filled his wrinkled face. "What can be so terrible that it brings shadows to your eyes?"

Zara gave her uncle a grateful look. "I have broken my engagement to Jacques, and the wedding is only three days away. What are we going to do?"

Megan heard Shafir's breath catch—it echoed her own shock. He rose to his feet, saying, "It doesn't matter. We will cancel it."

"But what about the celebrations, the concerts?" Zara glanced back at the king. "And what will we say to the people of Dhahara who have been looking forward to the wedding? I feel so terrible about letting everyone down."

Megan didn't envy Zara the anxiety and misery she was going through. But she couldn't help thinking that she'd had a lucky escape.

"Are you sure of this, Zara?" Rafiq asked. "Or is this nothing more than a squabble of lovebirds?"

"I am certain." Zara's voice rang out with conviction. "I do not want to marry a man who has another woman."

Megan felt the weight of Shafir's troubled gaze. Then he turned his attention back to Zara. "There may not be another woman, cousin."

"Oh, there is." Certainty sparked in her eyes. "Jacques has been seeing her every afternoon. He comes to visit me reeking of her."

There was a nasty silence.

The color drained out Megan's cheeks and she experienced a sinking sensation in the pit of her stomach.

They must think Zara was referring to *her.* But what

concerned her most was whether Shafir suspected her of sneaking out behind his back to meet with Jacques.

She wished she could see his eyes and assess for herself what he believed.

It took all her self-restraint to stop herself from leaping to her feet and yelling out, "It wasn't me."

Instead she sat and stared at her nails, awfully conscious of the undercurrents in the room, while of course Zara appeared blissfully oblivious.

"Zara, you might be mistaken," Khalid said half-heartedly.

"I am not! Jacques admitted everything. Her name is Rosie Smith, and she's an English tourist. And she's not the business colleague who's been stalking him. Jacques told me he met this woman less than a week ago."

Despite being aware of the discomfort of all the men, and despite Zara's misery, an indescribable relief swept through Megan.

At least Shafir now knew she hadn't being seeing Jacques on the sly.

"He told me he's found his soul mate." Zara sounded so bewildered that Megan's heart went out to her. "I always thought that was me."

A burst of annoyance caused Megan to say, "I wouldn't worry about it. There's no value in being his soul mate. It's an overused position."

All eyes turned to her.

Now she'd put her foot in it. For a brief space in time Megan wished she'd kept her mouth shut.

"He's a dog," said Shafir in a voice like steel. "You are well rid of him."

She glanced up and met his eyes and saw the summation was for her, as well as Zara. Shafir was right: Jacques was a dog. No doubt about it. And Zara had been saved much unhappiness. "I couldn't agree more."

He didn't smile, but his eyes were warm as they met hers. It gave her the strength she needed.

"There is something I have to say." She drew a ragged breath. "Zara, I came to Dhahara because of Jacques."

"You mean, Jacques invited you?"

"I'm the crazed colleague he told you was stalking him."

"You're that Megan?" The other woman's eyes went wide. "But—"

"He never told me he was engaged to you, that you were getting married in three weeks' time." Megan knew if she didn't get it all out now, she never would. Aware of Shafir standing tall and proud beside her, she focused on Zara.

"When he first told me he had business dealings with Dhahara, he kindled my interest in the country. When he suggested a short vacation together to get to know each other better—I insisted on going to Dhahara." Megan couldn't stop her lips curving upward. "Boy, he must have sweated about that."

"No, he thought he could get away with it. The arrogance of it!" Zara gave a snort of disgust. "He must think all women are stupid."

"He promised we would explore Dhahara and see if we had feelings for each other," Megan said. "No pressure."

"He said similar things to me, too. He was so romantic. I thought it was all for me."

"I know." Megan nodded. "And he's probably used the same script with this Rosie, too."

"I am so glad you told me that. I thought it was something that I'd done that made him stop loving me. My fault. That I wasn't woman enough for him."

"He's a serial adulterer," said Shafir with anger. "What woman would want such a man?"

"Not me," said Zara.

"Nor me," said Megan with a smile at the other woman.

"He's a rat," said Zara, warming to the theme.

"*Kalb*—a dog," growled Shafir.

"A rat-eating dog," said Zara with relish.

Mirth filled Megan. "A flea-infested, rat-eating dog."

The king laughed first, and everyone else followed suit.

When the hilarity was over, Rafiq said, "We will have to run the vermin out of town. And someone is going to have to let the people and the media know that there will be no wedding."

"I will," said Shafir. "And I must remember to tell the two tourism delegates I invited, too."

"That can all wait until tomorrow," said the king. "For tonight we will celebrate Zara's narrow escape. Ay me, when I think of how Zara might have suffered in the years to come..." He broke off and rubbed the bridge of his nose. Then his sharp black eyes rested on Megan. "I make my apologies to you, too, Megan, for any unhappiness you have endured. I can only say I am pleased that both you and Zara discovered what a weak character this man has."

"You see, that wasn't so bad," Shafir said, once they were back in the comfort of his home, as he poured Megan a cup of mint tea. Though it was nearly midnight, he'd made the offer of tea because she looked so wired he suspected the hot drink would help her to sleep.

She took the cup from him, cradling it between her hands and sank into the dark crimson sofa. "It was worse than bad, it was terrible. When Zara arrived..." Her voice trailed away and she shook her head at the memory.

"It saved me from the horns of a dilemma," said Shafir,

perching himself on the arm of the sofa. "Whether to tell Zara the truth, or to threaten Jacques with castration if he ever screwed around on Zara."

"Shafir, you savage!" But Megan couldn't stop the gurgle of laughter at the mental picture of his threatening Jacques.

"What do women see in him?" Shafir sounded driven.

She lifted one shoulder in a shrug and dropped it. "He's easy on the eyes."

Shafir snorted. "You and Zara are both intelligent women. The man must have something more than good looks."

It was not easy exposing her dreams. But Shafir was not the brute his reputation suggested. He listened. He understood. Most of the time. Perhaps he'd understand this, too.

She searched for the right words. "Jacques has a talent for homing in on what a woman most wants and saying what she most wants to hear. I wanted love—I suspect Zara was looking for that, too. The soul mate line worked. Jacques is charming. He courted me as if I were the only woman in the world for him. I started to believe it. Zara probably did, too."

It left a bitter taste in her mouth to realize how easily she'd been duped. "He was very convincing."

"I'm sure he was," he said abruptly.

"I wanted to fall in love. And he looked like he had all the right qualifications. He even knew about wine—and that's important to my family."

"And to you?" he asked quietly. "Is that essential?"

"All I want is someone who loves me more than anyone, anything in the world. You should see how my brothers look at the women they love. It's got nothing to do with what they do for a living. It's about who they are. Beloved."

Shafir slowly let out the breath he'd been holding.

Megan took another sip of tea. "Now that I've met your parents like you wanted, and now that Zara's not getting married, that means I'm free to go home, doesn't it?"

Her words resounded within him like the hollow knell of a heavy brass bell. "You don't have to go yet. You once said you'd come here seeking excitement, adventure, romance. Have you found all those?"

She shook her head slowly. "I was being flippant when I said that. Shafir, I can't stay. I need to get back home. There'll be tons of work to be done."

"You could come work here."

As he spoke, Shafir realized it offered a possible solution. A temporary solution until he convinced her how necessary she had become to him. But this way would buy him time, and he wouldn't lose her. Yet.

"I could do with someone like you."

"You don't grow wine," Megan pointed out, her pulse starting to pound at the thought of working with Shafir all day, every day.

"Don't be smart." He grinned at her, a glorious breathtaking grin, and her heart rolled over. "Your skills are easily transferable. There are aspects of my business I don't enjoy."

"So pay someone else to do it." He was a control freak, and she couldn't readily see him delegating stuff he considered important.

"I already do. But I find that they are not up to my expectations. I want you."

Her heart leaped at that. But he didn't mean it. Not in the way she wanted him to mean it.

"And you think I would be up to your expectations?" It was flattering that he wanted to hire her, and Megan found herself smiling across at him.

"Oh, yes, I'm quite sure of it. It's that boundless energy you have. Your enthusiasm for everything and everyone. Already you are catching on to Arabic. I heard the exchange you had with Naema early this morning."

Megan discovered she was actually considering his proposal. Don't, she told herself, it will only lead to heartache. She would always want more than he would ever be able to offer her.

She shifted under his intense stare. Time to be entertaining and lighten the mood. "Don't even think about it, Shafir."

"What?"

"Refusing to let me leave the country."

"Now there's a tempting thought." But he didn't look away, and Megan could feel the temperature rising.

She shouldn't even be considering staying...she really shouldn't.

"I can't," she said.

"I've gotten used to having you around." Shafir tried to make a joke of it. "Who's going to live in my harem at Qasr Al-Ward?"

Her expression was indeterminable. "I'm sure you'll have no difficulty filling the walled perfumed garden with throngs of women."

"I've never wanted throngs of women."

After a taut moment, she said, "What do you want?"

You. The truth of that was as fundamental to him as breathing. He wanted Megan forever. But after everything she'd been subjected to, he was quite sure she couldn't wait to get out of Dhahara.

As she was leaving regardless, it was worth one shot of honesty. "You want to know what I want right now? I want to carry you to my bed and forget all about tomorrow." About the wedding celebrations that needed to be cancelled, about booking Megan a ticket to the place she called home.

"Shafir—"

She was wavering.

"Please..." He held out his hand.

She set down the tiny cup she held and came to him.

He embraced her. She was soft and warm in his arms and a surge of protective strength filled him. Mine, he thought. My woman.

My wife…

A sense of rightness filled him. Megan was his. He wouldn't ask her to stay as his mistress, and she'd already refused his offer of employment. He had tonight to convince her that they belonged together as man and woman.

Shafir carried her up the empty stairs and down the corridor to his bedchamber. Once inside, he placed Megan gently on the bedcover of rich reds and purples.

But this time it wasn't about seduction; this time it was about infinitely more.

Leaning over, he kissed her neck, her cheeks, her lips. He worshipped her with his touch. She was silent. But her fingers stroked down his back, her touch telling him what words couldn't.

From there on everything moved quickly. Her clothes, his clothes, landed on the floor in a heap.

Her naked skin glowed like lustrous pearl in the pale glow of his bedside lamp. He stroked it, loving the silken softness. She undulated, and his hand repeated the movement starting at her shoulder, sliding over the sides of her breasts, across her belly, over her thighs, and retracing the path.

His lips followed where his fingers led. Megan arched up as his mouth explored the scented valley between her breasts. Moving lower, he tasted the sweetness of her inner thigh, and she moaned.

She was moist, ready. This time he was prepared. A moment's delay as he reached for the bed stand, then he moved over her and slid home. She was hot and wet and her arms came around him, pulling him into her. It was his turn to groan out loud.

He pressed forward, sinking down, then retreating. Her hips lifted slightly in response to each thrust, increasing the pleasure as their bodies moved as one.

The friction built, sensation spiraled upward, and Shafir shut his eyes as the heat took him. As he came, Megan gasped. He felt her contractions against him, and he fell through the veils of pleasure.

Megan lay back, gasping, blood pounding through her head. *Wow.* She tipped back her head to meet the eyes of the man balanced above her, who had taken her places she'd never been before.

Her soul mate.

The burnt bronze eyes were unexpectedly solemn. He reached out a hand and stroked her hair, his touch gentle, his fingers trembling.

He'd felt it, too.

Emotion washed through her, turning her limbs to water. "I don't think I'll be able to stand. I feel so weak." She tried to make light of the moment.

His lips curved into a smile, but his eyes remained intent. Her heart skipped a beat. What now?

"Megan, will you marry me?"

When it came, it shook her world. Her first thought was that she must have misheard him.

"What?"

"Will you do me the honor of becoming my wife, living with me at Qasr Al-Ward for all of our lives?"

"Shafir!"

He couldn't be serious. But there was no humor in his face, only implacable purpose.

He meant it.

He wanted her to marry him.

Oh, God.

"I can't."

The bronze dulled a little, but the determination in the set of his chin increased. "You can…if you choose to."

He slid over to the other side of the bed and she felt a shuddering sense of loss.

He pulled a sheet up over both of them and the loneliness eased.

Temptation tugged at her. It would be easy, so easy to give in, to be with him. "It's not about what I want. Surely you know that?"

He turned onto his side and propped his head up on his hand. "That's all it is about."

He was a desert prince. And even though her family was successful and wealthy, she was still a country girl at heart. His father had clear ideas of the kind of wife he needed, and she fell far short. How could she ever say yes?

"Your father is the king of Dhahara."

His mouth kinked and the laugh lines around his eyes deepened. "You won't be marrying my father. You'll be marrying me."

She played with the edge of the sheet. "But don't you see? You should marry someone suitable."

"I see someone who is eminently suitable. I see a woman who can inspire loyalty in a household, who can talk with a baker's wife and bargain in a busy *souk*. I see a woman who is not afraid to learn a complex, foreign language, or ride a camel, or make love in a life-affirming way. The woman I see is brave and talented and passionate. What more could I ever want?"

Her breath caught. "I say the wrong things… I open my mouth when I should keep it shut… I lose my temper. None of those are qualities you need in a wife. I'm not suitable."

But her heart was hammering in her chest, and Megan realized that she wanted more than anything in the world to say yes. The look in Shafir's eyes, his gravity, the tenderness in his touch when he'd made love to her, all of it made her believe that he loved her. It was almost more than she could bear.

He reached out a hand and touched her lips. "You tell the truth. There is not a sliver of deceit in you. That is a fine quality, one that I would be proud to have in my wife, not something to be ashamed about."

"I'm not a virgin."

He gave a dismissive shrug. "Nor am I."

Megan knew there was one more thing she needed to get out the way. But how would he react?

She took a deep breath. "I came to Dhahara to—"

He interrupted her. "Megan, I don't—"

"Don't." She held up a hand. "Please don't stop me. I need to say this. If there is ever to be a way clear for us, we need to talk about Jacques. I came here to fall in love with him. Will you be able to live all our lives with the knowledge that even though I was never his lover, I came here to do my best to fall in love with another man?"

His breath caught at the admission that she and Jacques had never been lovers. She knew then that he would never have asked, and the softening in his mouth told her of his relief.

"And I had the task of keeping you away from him. I abducted you, locked you away. Will you be able to live with that?"

She took the hand that lay on the sheets and held it between both of hers. "I will thank you every day of our lives that you saved me from a horrible mistake."

"I don't believe you would have fallen in love with him."

"No, because I love you."

His eyes blazed. "That is all that matters." He swept her into his arms and kissed her until she had no breath left.

When he finally released her, she said, "We both need time."

He shook his head. "If you agree, I want to be married as soon as possible."

"Be reasonable," she pleaded.

"I am being reasonable. I don't give a fig about Garnier. About what my family thinks. All I care about is you. Haven't you realized that yet?" The intensity of his regard caused something to splinter deep in her heart. "In fact, if I had more grace I would thank Garnier for bringing you to Dhahara, for bringing us together, woman for whom I shall forsake all others."

Moved beyond measure, Megan burrowed deeper into him. "We would have met," she said at last. "You are my destiny."

"So you will marry me?"

"If you insist."

"I do."

I do.

The words had become a steady refrain over the past three days, Shafir realized with some satisfaction.

There had been the press conference. "You want to get married, Your Highness?" That had come from a stunned news reporter.

"I do."

Then her family had arrived in full force. There had been the interrogation by her three brothers, Joshua, Rafaelo and Heath, which had ended in one question: "Do you love Megan?"

"I do," he had replied.

Her mother and father had beamed with relief. Her

brothers had shaken Shafir's hand, their grip warning him that they would be expecting him to take excellent care of their baby sister.

Shafir had no intention of doing anything else.

Finally their women had hugged Megan and wished her every happiness.

And now there was the wedding. The most important "I do" moment of them all.

He'd wanted to get married immediately. But first he'd had to convince Megan.

It had taken some doing.

He'd argued that there was no need to wait—a wedding was ready to roll. What was the point of wasting a state wedding that had already been arranged?

She'd paled. "It's too grand."

"I am a royal prince. The people of Dhahara can't wait for a wedding."

"There's not enough time," she'd wailed.

"For what? We've already made all the important decisions." Like that he loved her. And she loved him.

"For a dress."

He'd laughed then. "That can be done in a day."

"To make a guest list."

"The invites went out months ago for Zara and Jacques. Sure, some of those people will drop off and you'll have some of your own guests, but it can be done." Fortunately her family and closest friends had dropped everything and flown here.

"I need time to study that list, to familiarize myself with the names so I can talk sense to your guests. It's a state occasion."

"I don't care about anyone else. You'll be talking to me. It's our wedding day."

"I need time to think."

That was the one thing he wasn't giving her. And now as she stood beside him in a stunning white silk wedding dress he was very pleased that he hadn't.

The dazed look that she'd worn over the past two days had at last subsided. He couldn't wait for the wedding to be over and to see her laugh again. Joie de vivre. He gave her hand a gentle squeeze as he prepared himself to say the words that had become the cornerstone of his life over the past few days.

I do.

I do love you.

I do cherish you.

I do forsake all others.

Forever.

His eyes met Megan's as he spoke the vows of his heart.

He forgot about the people watching—his family, her family. He forgot about the fact that the wedding was being televised for the people of his land. He forgot about everything except the woman who stood beside him.

His bride.

It was late.

The fireworks were over. Katar rested as Malik drove the limousine back to King Selim's palace where the reception had been hosted.

Shafir pulled his wife across the long seat of the limousine into his arms. "Happy?"

She tilted her head up. "Oh, yes."

Tomorrow they would return to Qasr Al-Ward. Shafir planned to take Megan deep into the desert for a few nights of time alone. But tonight they would spend in his city residence.

"I was surprised by how many people congratulated me today." She glanced up at him through her lashes. "There seemed to be a view that you were too wild for any woman to wed."

Shafir started to laugh.

"Several people expressed pity and told me that I'd have to get used to living in the desert. I told them that I came to Dhahara in search of excitement, adventure and romance."

The laughter faded from his face, and a gleam of concern lit his eyes. "Does that worry you? If it does, we can spend more time in the city."

"That would be like caging a tiger." She paused, examining her husband. "The first time I met you I decided you were untamed. Wild. A man who could never be civilized."

"A savage." His teeth flashed in the dimness.

"My savage. And it's that raw male strength that's exactly what I love. My soul mate. You're everything I ever wanted."

"You are the wife of my desert heart—my *ain.*My only one."

Megan's breath caught at his whispered words. He bent his head to kiss her, and for a few minutes there was silence.

When he raised his head, he said, "I have a wedding gift waiting for you at Qasr Al-Ward."

"A wedding gift?"

"It's not the usual jewels—although I'll buy you those, too," he added hastily. "This is something that I think no other woman would value as much as you will."

Megan tipped her head to one side. "What is it?"

"I should make you wait and see so that it's a surprise."

"Tell me!"

"It's a camel."

He watched in amusement as her eyes grew bright, her face filled with joy and she started to laugh.

"You bought the little white camel from the breeder you called a jerk, didn't you?"

He inclined his head. "You know me better than I know myself."

She threw herself against his chest and tilted her face up to his, her eyes dancing. "Now I know you love me. And I also know that you always intended for me to return to Qasr Al-Ward."

"Well, I never did show you the palmerie I planted."

She gave him a slow, secret smile. "No, I was going to remind you about that before I left."

"But now you're not leaving." There was a wealth of satisfaction in the statement.

Megan snuggled up to him. "My home is where you are."

"Tonight, home will be in Katar, and tomorrow let us go to Qasr Al-Wadi." Shafir smiled and closed his arms around her.

He'd waited too long for this joy. Now it was his.

* * * * *

Don't miss Tessa Radley's next Desire novel,
Part of the BILLIONAIRES AND BABIES promotion
On sale August 11, 2009 from Silhouette Desire.

*Celebrate 60 years of pure reading pleasure
with Harlequin®!*

*Step back in time and enjoy a sneak preview of an
exciting anthology from Harlequin® Historical with
THE DIAMONDS OF WELBOURNE MANOR.*

This compelling anthology features three stories about
the outrageous Fitzmanning sisters. Meet Annalise,
who is never at a loss for words… But that can change
with an unexpected encounter in the forest.

Available May 2009 from Harlequin® Historical.

"I'm the illegitimate daughter of notoriously scandalous parents, Mr. Milford. Candidates for my hand are unlikely to be lining up at the gates."

"Don't be so quick to discount your charms, my dear. Or the charm of your substantial dowry. Or even your brothers' influence. There are as many reasons to marry as there are marriages."

Annalise snorted. "Oh, yes. Perhaps I shall marry for dynastic reasons, or perhaps for property or influence. After all, a loveless, practical marriage worked out so well for my mother."

"Well, you've routed me on that one. I can think of no suitable rejoinder." Ned rose to his feet and extended his hand. "And since that is the case, let me be the first to wish you a long and happy spinsterhood."

Her mouth gaped open. And then she laughed.

And he froze.

This was the first time, Ned realized. The first time he'd seen her eyes light up and her mouth curl. The first time he'd witnessed her features melded together in glorious accord to produce exquisite beauty.

Unbelievable what a change came over her face. Unheard of what effect her throaty, rasping laughter had on his body. It pounded a beat upon his ear, quickly taken up by his pulse. It echoed through him, finally residing in his stirring nether regions.

So easily she did it, awakened these sensations within him—without any apparent effort at all. And she had called him potentially dangerous? Clearly the intelligent thing for him to do would be to steer clear, to leave her to the tender ministrations of Lord Peter Blackthorne.

"You were right." She smiled up at him as she took his hand and climbed to her feet. "I do feel better."

Ah, well. When had he ever chosen the intelligent path?

He did not relinquish her hand. He used it to pull her in, close enough that he could feel the warmth of her. "At the risk of repeating Lord Peter's mistake and anticipating too much—may I ask if you'll be my partner in battledore tomorrow?"

Her smile dimmed. Her breath came a little faster. His own had gone shallow, as if he'd just run a race—and lost. He ran his gaze over the appealing lift of her brow and the curious angle of her chin. His index finger twitched.

"I should like that," she said.

His finger trembled again and he lifted it, traced the pink and tender shell of her ear, the unique sweep of her jaw. Her pulse leaped beneath her skin, triggering his own. Slowly he tilted her chin up, waiting for her to object, to step back, to slap his hand away.

She did none of those eminently sensible things. Which left him free to do the entirely impractical thing.

Baby soft, the skin of her lips. Her whole body trembled when he touched her there.

He leaned in. Her eyes closed, even as she stood straight against him, strung as tight as a bow. He pressed his mouth to hers. It was a soft kiss, sweet and chaste. And yet he was hot and hard and as ready as he'd ever been in his life.

She drew back a little. Sighed. Their breath mingled a moment before she slowly backed away.

"Oh," she breathed. Her dark eyes were full of wonder and something that looked like fear. He took a step toward her, but she only shook her head. His outstretched hand fell to his side as she turned to disappear into the wood. This was the first time, Ned realized. The first time, since he'd come to the house party at Welbourne Manor, that he'd seen her eyes light up.

* * * * *

Follow Ned and Annalise's story in May 2009 in
THE DIAMONDS OF WELBOURNE MANOR.
Available May 2009 from Harlequin® Historical.

Available in the series romance section, or in the
historical romance section, wherever books are sold.

**We'll be spotlighting a different series
every month throughout 2009
to celebrate our 60th anniversary.**

Look for Harlequin® Historical in May!

Celebrations begin with
a sumptuous Regency house party!

Join three scandalous sisters in

**THE DIAMONDS OF
WELBOURNE MANOR**

Glittering, scintillating, sensual fun
by Diane Gaston, Deb Marlowe
and Amanda McCabe.

**60 years of Harlequin,
600 years of romance
in Harlequin Historical!**

www.eHarlequin.com   HHBPA09

The Inside Romance newsletter has a NEW look for the new year!

Same great content, brand-new look!

The Inside Romance newsletter is a FREE quarterly newsletter highlighting our upcoming series releases and promotions!

Click on the Inside Romance link on the front page of **www.eHarlequin.com** or e-mail us at insideromance@harlequin.ca to sign up to receive your FREE newsletter today!

You can also subscribe by writing to us at: HARLEQUIN BOOKS Attention: Customer Service Department P.O. Box 9057, Buffalo, NY 14269-9057

Please allow 4-6 weeks for delivery of the first issue by mail.

REQUEST YOUR FREE BOOKS!

2 FREE NOVELS PLUS 2 FREE GIFTS!

Silhouette® *Desire*®

Passionate, Powerful, Provocative!

YES! Please send me 2 FREE Silhouette Desire® novels and my 2 FREE gifts (gifts are worth about $10). After receiving them, if I don't wish to receive any more books, I can return the shipping statement marked "cancel". If I don't cancel, I will receive 6 brand-new novels every month and be billed just $4.05 per book in the U.S. or $4.74 per book in Canada. That's a savings of almost 15% off the cover price! It's quite a bargain! Shipping and handling is just 25¢ per book*. I understand that accepting the 2 free books and gifts places me under no obligation to buy anything. I can always return a shipment and cancel at any time. Even if I never buy another book, the two free books and gifts are mine to keep forever.

225 SDN ERVX   326 SDN ERVM

Name	(PLEASE PRINT)
Address	Apt. #
City	State/Prov. Zip/Postal Code

Signature (if under 18, a parent or guardian must sign)

Mail to the Silhouette Reader Service:
IN U.S.A.: P.O. Box 1867, Buffalo, NY 14240-1867
IN CANADA: P.O. Box 609, Fort Erie, Ontario L2A 5X3

Not valid to current subscribers of Silhouette Desire books.

Want to try two free books from another line?
Call 1-800-873-8635 or visit www.morefreebooks.com.

* Terms and prices subject to change without notice. Prices do not include applicable taxes. Sales tax applicable in N.Y. Canadian residents will be charged applicable provincial taxes and GST. Offer not valid in Quebec. This offer is limited to one order per household. All orders subject to approval. Credit or debit balances in a customer's account(s) may be offset by any other outstanding balance owed by or to the customer. Please allow 4 to 6 weeks for delivery. Offer available while quantities last.

Your Privacy: Silhouette Books is committed to protecting your privacy. Our Privacy Policy is available online at www.eHarlequin.com or upon request from the Reader Service. From time to time we make our lists of customers available to reputable third parties who may have a product or service of interest to you. If you would prefer we not share your name and address, please check here. ☐

SDES09